The bullet hit him in the shoulder and threw him to the ground...

The Executioner looked at the wound. Bad. Blood all over his arm. Blood dripping down his fingers. Too much blood.

He cursed against the pain. Still holding the AK-47, he stumbled back into the trench. He was blinded by blood and dizziness.

The woman in the trench gasped when she saw his wound. She grabbed a rifle and peered over the edge at the enemy.

"Stay down!" Bolan shouted.

She turned to look at him and a single round hit her head. It slapped her backward into the trench. Bolan stared at the woman. Her eyes were closed, and the whole side of her head was bloody.

He roared in anger and fury. He launched himself over the top of the trench, emptying his magazine in a wild rage.

Now nothing would live!

MACK BOLAN
The Executioner

DON PENDLETON's EXECUTIONER

MACK BOLAN

Hellbinder

A GOLD EAGLE BOOK FROM

WORLDWIDE

TORONTO · NEW YORK · LONDON · PARIS
AMSTERDAM · STOCKHOLM · HAMBURG
ATHENS · MILAN · TOKYO · SYDNEY

First edition December 1984

ISBN 0-373-61072-6

Special thanks and acknowledgment to
Chet Cunningham for his contributions to this work.

Printed in Canada

The courage we desire and prize is not the courage to die decently but to live manfully.
—*Thomas Carlyle*

Violence and brutality are not the same.
Only a man of courage will know the difference.
—*Mack Bolan*

Dedicated to the victims of
chemical war, who have been ravaged by
the effects of bacteriological
and chemical weapons.

1

Mack Bolan heard the whispers of the three silenced rounds as they passed inches over his head. He rolled to one side and stared through the grass at the other man's position. He had seen the muzzle flash, faint through the silencer but still visible.

In the soft, dark silence, Bolan heard the *thonk* of a two-way radio transmission button being pushed into the send mode. At once the Executioner sent two 3-round bursts from his silenced Beretta 93-R into the shielded position thirty yards below him.

Before the sound of casings flipping from the machine pistol died, the black-suited nightfighter sensed movement behind him. He turned and saw a form on the skyline, saw it duck behind some bushes.

Bolan did not move or breathe. Again he sensed the man behind him stir, then the soft *snic* of metal slipping past metal. He dived away from the sound, hit the dirt, held the Beretta to his chest and rolled a dozen times. Four seconds later the woodsy knoll near where he had been lying erupted with a grenade's shattering roar. Deadly shards of steel exploded in all directions, shredding leaves, digging into the tree trunk, and a few sailing angrily over

Bolan's head where he was pressed against the soft ground.

Bolan stood and ran hard for the position he had pinpointed ahead. He could see that it was a dug-in foxhole, a concealed outpost straight out of an infantry field manual. His target would stay there; the guy had orders and nowhere to retreat. Bolan put three single shots into the parapet around the hole as he ran, then stopped abruptly by the four-foot-deep foxhole.

A snarl by the surprised guard came too late as Bolan fired a 3-round burst from the Beretta, sending the 9mm parabellums crashing through the man's chest, pulping his heart and driving him into the bottom of the ready-made grave, cheating the undertaker of a fee.

The deathbringer picked up the foot-long hand-held radio, then ran toward the road, away from the fragger man in the brush. He had found out what he wanted to know. Here was a hardsite, with plenty of external protection in a rural area forty miles outside Boise, Idaho. He retreated until he was a quarter mile from the buildings, which he had seen were all that remained of a once thriving dairy business.

Bolan's nightscope showed him more details.

The main house was surrounded by a six-foot chain link fence.

Two Doberman pinscher attack dogs patrolled inside the wire.

A special shortwave antenna was mounted on the farmhouse roof.

Night safety lights had snapped on when the grenade exploded, and they now illuminated three sides of the house.

A guard with a submachine gun walked a post in front of the house, outside the fence.

Bolan studied all these factors. He decided against taking on the place tonight with his one machine pistol.

The Executioner put the scope away and lay in the grass, watching. He wondered how long they would keep the lights on. He was not ready to leave without making a larger impression on them, and especially on Aleksandr Galkin, a Class Four KGB Field Agent who had lived in the United States for six years. He was the agent in charge in Boise. His name was high on the list of secret KGB operatives that Bolan had stolen in Moscow, on which notations suggested that this would be a two-man post soon to be involved in an unspecified project.

An hour later the small two-way radio he captured had still not been used by the enemy. He saw one man come from the hill, enter a locked front gate and go into the house. Then a half hour later the floodlights went off. In the moonlight, Bolan could see the guard moving along his beat in front of the safehouse.

Deciding to question the man, the black-clad warrior moved like a swift shadow down the hill, across the open area near the side of the house and forward toward the guard.

He heard faint music. Was it from the house? The sound came closer and louder. Walking his beat, the guard held a small transistor radio to his ear. The spillover was what the Executioner heard in the otherwise silent countryside. In Chicago or New York City or even Omaha the sound would be gobbled up. Here it stood out plainly.

The nightfighter lay in tall grass twenty feet from the fence around the safehouse. He heard another noise and two black forms surged silently along the fence, like twin demons. Only the bared fangs of the Dobermans showed through the darkness.

"Vnis! Tikhi!" the guard snapped at the dogs. They turned and padded softly the other way.

Bolan dredged up his Russian; the words meant "Down! Quiet!" So either the guard was Russian, or he knew the language. Finding out which would be interesting.

The guard watched the dogs a moment, then turned and walked his route to the other side of the house. Knowing that the noise of the guard's movements would cover his own, Bolan crawled toward a thick concrete post in the fence and rested where the fence made a square turn around the side of the house. The Executioner lay just out of sight of the guard. He angled the Beretta upward.

The guard walked to the end of his beat and returned, the small AM radio still to his ear. As he neared, Bolan noted that he was medium height, of stocky build, and wore a shirt and heavy plaid jacket against the autumn chill. He carried a short automatic weapon, probably a Heckler & Koch, slung over his shoulder.

When the guard came to the end of his route he

was fewer than three feet from Bolan's head, which was screened by the heavy wire fence and the thick concrete post. Bolan kneeled as soon as the guard turned away from the house, then stood and carefully extended a stainless-steel wire noose attached to a three-foot steel rod. The noose encircled the guard's head and Bolan jerked the rod, drawing the noose tight, slightly puncturing the skin around the guard's throat. The man dropped his weapon, clawed frantically at the deadly wire and grabbed for his attacker, but no one was within reach.

Bolan stepped back, pulling the steel rod and his catch with him. The guard tried to shout: the wire bit deeper into his throat and only a strangled gurgle emerged. Bolan jerked the pole and the guard moved toward him. Then Bolan tugged his prize catch into the tall grass twenty yards to the side of the house.

The Executioner held the garrote tightly around the neck of his prisoner, forcing him down into the grass. Finally he eased the pressure and pushed the Beretta into the man's cheek. He looked young, no more than a kid.

"Not a sound except to answer my questions, understand?" The guard's eyes were wild with pain and fright. He nodded.

Bolan eased the steel pole down but held it ready. The guard moved his head gently, took a deep breath.

"What do you want to know?" It was a mid-American drawl with a slight Western twang.

"How many men inside?"

"Right now, six."

"How much security outside?"

"You're the guy they threw that fragger at! Lew was on the radio, said he pitched one at somebody shooting. There's just three of us out here."

"None now. Lew is inside, the one in the foxhole is dead, and you're on your way out. That leaves none. Is Galkin inside, Aleksandr Galkin?"

"Yeah, there's a guy name of Galkin. They call him Al."

"Any more men coming soon?"

"I just signed on yesterday to walk guard duty out here. I don't know anything about any of this. You CIA or something?"

"Something. What is Al doing here?"

"Didn't say. I'm a soldier of fortune. Work for anybody who pays me to pack a gun."

"Even these KGB killers?"

"Hey, they ain't KGB! They ain't Russian."

"Then why all the security here?"

"Didn't say. I didn't ask."

"Why were you talking to the dogs in Russian?"

"They told me to. They said those were the only words the dogs knew."

"You're too stupid to be lying." Bolan took the guard's hidden .32 automatic, then gently removed the steel wire from around his throat.

"You want to go on living?"

"Yeah."

"I hope you're that smart. You got wheels?"

"That's my Honda 250 over by the trees."

"Get on it and gun out of here. I mean, make lots of noise."

"They'll shoot me."

"Maybe. If you don't try it, I'll kill you right here."

The young man jumped to his feet and ran. Bolan's Beretta tracked him to the trees. A moment later the Honda motorcycle sputtered, then roared into action. It varoomed three times. The kid gunned it again and headed down the lane.

The exterior floodlights came on. The Executioner ducked lower in the tall grass. Three rifle shots followed the bike rider but the bike kept going.

Bolan watched the house. Lights inside snapped on. He heard voices. A door banged. Then an outside door burst open and a man ran to the inside gate, out and around to the front. He watched the dark landscape for a moment, then slung his automatic weapon over his shoulder and began to walk along the fence.

The Executioner waited, giving the man time to lower his watchfulness. Two shadows flittered around the inside of the fence, white fangs moving through the blackness.

Five minutes later the silent warrior had returned to the corner of the fence, timing his move so the wandering black demons would be on the far side of the compound in their regular movements around the wire.

The new sentry was smaller, maybe five-nine. He was also more alert. He saw Bolan and swung his automatic weapon on target, muttering a string of Russian curses. Only a round from the silenced Beretta stopped him. The hot lead slanted off the guard's H&K and tore into his shoulder; he dropped the weapon and groaned. The nightfighter surged upward and knocked the guy down, the Beretta smashing hard beside his ear. The man had to be Russian. Nobody learns to swear like that in a stateside Russian-language class. Bolan was especially alert now, expecting trouble.

The two dogs made no noise as they padded toward him across the fence.

The guard was unconscious. Bolan found only a candy bar in the guy's pockets. Two sets of gleaming eyes watched the black-clad man through the wire. Lights came on inside. A shout spoiled the countryside quiet. Someone else called in Russian from behind the house.

Bolan hoisted the unconscious guard above his head, then pushed him over the six-foot wire fence so that he fell into the compound.

This time there was no command given to the dogs. They leaped silently at the guard. The first Doberman's jaws clamped around the guard's throat, then pulled, taking out both carotid arteries. The second Doberman's big fangs tore at the man's head a dozen slashing times. A moment later both dogs backed away. The smell of death stopped their attack. They whined softly and continued their patrol around the fence.

Just then the floodlights turned on. Bolan was still in their glare. He ran away from them, heard a pistol crack behind him, dived and rolled into the darkness, then was up and running hard again, zig-zagging through the soft moonlight toward the woods on the upslope away from the old dairy farm.

Two down, one gone. That should leave five at the safehouse, if the motorcycle kid knew what he was talking about.

They would have to wait until tomorrow. He would need some heavy gear to blast his way inside. Tomorrow night, or perhaps the next morning.

As he ran through the woods he heard a car coming down the half-mile lane between the gravel road and the old farm. Reinforcements, or more of the regular staff? How many men did Aleksandr need in Idaho? Bolan stopped and watched the car come to a halt at the security fence. Now he could see six or seven men around the body of the guard. The dogs killed him, they would know that.

But they would do all sorts of wondering about who shot him and pushed him over the fence.

2

Aleksandr Galkin stared at the bloody, dog-chewed face and neck of his number-three man. "Everyone inside at once!" he commanded. "Put the car behind the old barn! All security lights on until dawn. First watch three hours, second watch to dawn. Let's go!"

The group followed Aleksandr inside. He was not a tall man, more in the mold of other forty-year-old KGB men. A little over five feet ten and—his doctor told him—thirty pounds overweight. He always dressed meticulously and now wore a light gray sweater and Sansabelt slacks of a contrasting shade of gray. He ran his hand over a widow's peak that was losing its fight to maintain the forehead hair.

"Two men dead and we have not even seen our attacker! An automatic weapon was used, so that rules out the police. The CIA is not supposed to operate within the United States, so who is it? Our local contacts tell us the FBI is not involved at all in this area." He was speaking to the five men he had carefully recruited and trained.

"There is no possible way we can alter our schedule," he continued. "We will move against the target as you have been instructed. We need three new men to be trained thoroughly, starting right now. I know it is late. As we are on guard, we will also be training these new men and retraining the rest of you.''

He looked at the men standing in what once had been the farmhouse living room. The furniture had been pushed back and seven folding chairs arranged in front of a standing blackboard. Aleksandr motioned to Sergei Vinogradov, his number two and the man qualified to carry through if Aleksandr himself died early in the operation.

"Sergei, round up the three new men."

Within minutes, Vinogradov returned with the three men. Aleksandr excused the other five and put one on watch at the window of a darkened room at the front of the house. The leader looked at his new men and scowled.

"This is not a suicide mission. I fully expect to go into the target with six men and to come out with all six of us. It is a matter of training, discipline and knowledge. All of us will do exactly as we are directed, complete our part in the mission and move to the appointed place for transport, whether by our own vehicle or the choppers. For you new men I will take this from the beginning.''

He poured a cup of coffee from a vacuum coffeepot and watched the men. Two had been working with him on minor jobs for a year, the third was a recruit. Aleksandr hated to work this close to the deadline with new men, but it did have some advantages.

''As you have been told, you are committed.

There are no leaves or vacations. You will be here until the mission is over. You will each receive the stipulated ten thousand dollars. If you are wounded, your medical expenses will be covered completely. In the off-chance of a death, your family will be compensated with fifty thousand dollars. Are there any questions about this aspect?"

None of the men responded.

"Moving on. When we attack we will go in softly and quietly, attack with deadly effect and accomplish our mission. We have a set timetable and no more than sixty seconds plus or minus will be allowed for the total mission."

He swung up the cover on a chart that had been draped over the blackboard.

"Here is the target, the Binder Chemical Corporation. That is exactly what it looks like—a chemical processor, producer and distributor. In actuality it is much more. The site is ten miles from the little town of Emmett and more than five miles from the closest farm family. The reasoning was to safeguard the civilian population in case of chemical accident.

"The day after tomorrow there will be one of those accidents, and we will make it worse. For your information, this target is not a simple business, but one of the most secret and highly defended facilities in the United States. In the ten stories of underground vaults, rooms and tunnels, the U.S. government has stored more than fifty percent of the nation's ready-to-use chemical and biological warfare substances.

"Now for a schematic of the area and the facility." Aleksandr turned over another page of the chart to reveal an artist's rendering of the outside of the Binder Chemical Corporation. It was two stories high, with no windows on the ground floor and few on the second. An overhead view showed that the building was in the shape of a huge, hollow square. Spur rail lines came up to two sides. Aleksandr touched the inside of the square.

"From one side of the open area to the other is just over two hundred feet. It's a big place. But it is even larger underground."

He turned over another sheet. It showed a side drawing of a ten-level complex. His pointer ticked off the important points.

"The two floors above ground are mostly administrative and living quarters for the military and scientific personnel. They are also for show, to establish the business front of the place. The communications room is here, along with the power supply switching station and quarters for some security people.

"In the switching station, the master control console is arranged so the levels can be shut off from all electrical power one subfloor at a time. We appreciate that help.

"Level Sub One, or S-1, is mostly administrative, housekeeping and more security.

"S-2 is for moderate chemical warfare devices. Some of the older gases, tear and nausea gases of all types, and some of the less virulent bacteriological seed cultures that must be kept under constant heat and humidity controls are all stored here in rooms. There are vaults, freezers, and some of the toxins are even in ovens. We will neutralize any personnel here and bypass the subfloor.

"S-3 is for the more extreme types of nerve gases and the more sensitive bacteriological strains and cultures.

"S-4 is our target. Here the most destructive and deadly nerve gases are stored. We don't want all the supply, only six canisters of the best!"

He smiled and dropped the cover over the chart. "The people in the complex will attempt to stop us from taking the six tanks. That is their job. We will see if our small, expert force is better than their much larger but ill-equipped, poorly trained and less determined group. We will see ourselves win.

"That's enough for now. You'll receive six hours of detailed instruction tomorrow about exactly what you are to do, how you will do it and what we do when we come out of the hole with the canisters.

"Now get to your bunks in the basement. You'll be up at 3:00 A.M. for guard duty."

The three men looked serious as they left. There was none of the light camaraderie shared by true soldiers after a briefing.

Aleksandr went to the only room without a window on the first floor and sat heavily in the soft chair. He mixed a drink and leaned back.

Two more days and his greatest adventure would begin. He had come a long way in the KGB. There had been no family connections for him. He had not been included in those chosen to go to the Institute for International Studies, which would have given him quick entry into the KGB. Instead he had to spend four years in the army, apply three times and pass tough tests before being accepted for training. He had begun at the bottom, worked twice as hard as anyone else and had at last been promoted to field rank.

But even here he did not find the thrill, the danger, the life-and-death contests he wanted. He watched other agents make modest successes and return to Moscow and move slowly ahead in the party and the KGB organization. He had no such ambition. He was working toward exactly what he wanted now. His instructions had been to steal one of the canisters of the nerve gas. But while he was at the store he might as well help himself to five more of the deadly canisters. He had contacts who were delighted to have such a product available. They knew exactly how to use it, and would pay handsomely.

Aleksandr smiled, and sipped the drink. Those plans for the other five canisters had nothing to do with the party, Mother Russia or the KGB.

If everything went well he would be leaving the KGB service, but not before he set up his own "accidental" death deep in the jungles of Central America. And before this he would finalize the arrangements that would make him a millionaire, that would establish him with a wealthy man's life-style for the rest of his days, in any country he wished to live. He could even go back to Moscow with new identity papers and passport from anywhere. He would need a slightly different face and a new set of fingerprints, but what a thrill that would be.

Aleksandr shivered as he looked out at the lights surrounding the sturdy fence. It would not be long now. Not long at all!

3

Mack Bolan woke up at 5:30 A.M. as usual and did one hundred pushups and one hundred situps. He ran two miles down the highway and back. Then he showered and dressed in his three-piece business suit for the day. It was Saturday, but he had phoned the previous afternoon and discovered that Binder Chemical Corporation was open Saturday morning.

Bolan had spent most of Friday tailing suspects from the safehouse. Two of them had parked near the chemical firm.

Now he bought a plastic envelope with a zipper on top to serve as a minibriefcase. He filled it with samples of business forms he bought at the same stationery store, and drove the ten miles to the company building. He parked in one of the few spaces for visitors and walked into Binder Chemicals shortly after 9:00 A.M.

Inside the entrance an attractive, well-dressed young woman looked up from her desk. "Good morning, sir. How may we help you?" she asked pleasantly.

"Maxwell Bond," Bolan said. "Commercial Printing Corporation. We specialize in business forms. Now if I could talk with your purchasing agent or your supervisor in charge of office supplies, I'm sure that I can save your company five or six thousand dollars a year.''

The brown-eyed blonde listened attentively, a sly smile shadowing her pretty face.

"Oh, I'm sorry. I bet you could save us lots of money. But I'm afraid no one from those departments is available. Would you like to come back Monday?''

"I have to be in Boise on Monday—appointments all day long.''

As Bolan stood there, seemingly dejected, he took an exacting inventory of the place. A maintenance man had appeared shortly after Bolan's arrival, and was sweeping a small area near the far doors. He had Security Guard written all over him. His short haircut seemed out of place for a modern business.

On the opposite side of the entrance, two young men emerged from an elevator. Both were trim, wore business suits and also had short haircuts. They stood and talked about some business operation, and neither looked toward Bolan.

"Well, miss, I'm stumped. Could I maybe leave some material for your manager to look at?''

"Yes, of course, Mr. Bond. You can leave samples for our manager. But I know that he just did some ordering last month.''

"What about taking your manager to lunch?'' Bolan said. "He has to eat and it would be a chance to talk over...." Bolan's voice faded as the girl shook her head.

"I'm sorry, but he can't. He always takes a ten-mile run at lunchtime. A real health nut."

"Looks like I struck out."

"I'm sorry. Try again in six months." She smiled again.

"Thanks for your help. Maybe in six months then." The Executioner examined a small display case and several pictures of the company's operation on the walls. The two young men were joined by a third, and as one turned, the outline of a shoulder rig and a gun became visible under his left arm. Security all over the place.

Bolan waved to the receptionist, left the building, walked straight to his camper and drove away. He felt eyes on him all the time. He had felt a tension as soon as he had entered the building. This was not a simple chemical plant.

He drove the ten miles back to Emmett and stopped at a telephone booth. He used his Calling Card and phoned the special number in Virginia, the only phone in the Stony Man complex that was not on automatic record, the only one Mack Bolan ever called.

When it rang, Aaron "The Bear" Kurtzman answered.

Kurtzman had been seriously wounded in an attack on the Appalachian mountain hardsite that had been Bolan's headquarters when Bolan was known as Colonel John Phoenix, counterterrorist. Kurtzman now was limited to a wheelchair, paralyzed from the waist down. But his hands and his mind were as active as ever.

"Bear? This is a friend. How's it going?"

He recognized Bolan's voice at once. The warmth was almost tangible. "It's good to hear from you again. Are you well?"

"I'm fine, Bear, but I need a small favor." Bolan quickly described the target of his curiosity, the Binder Chemical Corporation. Kurtzman grunted.

"I think I know what the place is, but let me double-check. Hold the line."

Bolan imagined Kurtzman wheeling over to his favorite computer and punching in the question. The answer would arrive within microseconds.

"That's a touchy one," Kurtzman said forty seconds later. "I had to go through three clearances just to get the name from the memory banks. The Binder Depository is ten underground levels storing more than half of our stockpile of biological and chemical weapons, cultures and assorted secrets. It is disguised as a civilian firm. It should by rights have an Army armored division around it, but a code here reveals the military's thinking. They figure if nobody knows it's there, nobody can hurt it. Sounds like you're onto something big, my friend."

"Not me. I don't work for Uncle anymore. I retired. Just trying to retire some KGB agents."

"I know how you feel. Listen, it's the real stuff where you are. Be careful."

"Always. And as we used to say, stay hard."

Bolan got in his camper and drove. He considered his weapons. A friendly contact had set him up with a good supply of hardware. For a change he had all the armament he could use, including a Redeye Army shoulder-held missile launcher that could punch a hole in a cement building.

The Redeye, the Army's M-41E1, was designed to allow infantrymen to shoot down low-flying jet aircraft. It was designed for heat-seeking and homing missiles, but had been adapted for straight explosive missiles with the punch of a big howitzer.

Everything else Bolan needed was in the camper. Three miles from the farmhouse, he backed the vehicle into a lane with heavy brush, out of sight of the road. He field-stripped and cleaned all the weapons he would use the next day, including the big .44 AutoMag, his Beretta 93-R with its 15-round magazine and a lightweight Childers Automatic Combat Shotgun that could pump out twenty rounds of double O buck in six seconds.

When all were oiled and returned to their hidden storage spots, he looked over the Redeye. A simple device, it was a big improvement over the old bazooka, and its small rocket missiles had a range of more than two miles. He had four straight HE rounds, not heat-seeking. At three hundred yards they would work wonders.

Bolan put the Beretta in its belt holster under his light jacket and walked along the road through the woods. A mile down, he cut across a pasture to a small stream and followed the cover the willows and brush provided. Downstream another mile he climbed a small hill and just over the brow looked down at the farmhouse that had become a Soviet safehouse.

He was a half mile away and sure their security would not extend this far. The access road was from the opposite side of the hill; evidently this area had been used for pasture when the dairy was flourishing. Now it was a natural grassland with a few trees.

Quickly he chose his attack site, more than a quarter mile beyond his present position. A small knoll on the hill would provide enough protection from the front, yet allow the back blast of the Redeye to dissipate without pinpointing his position. He figured it would take three shots: the first to get the range, the second to hit the front door, the third for the fence. Then he would charge with assault fire, storm into the place with the Childers slamming death pellets into anything that moved.

He lay there watching the target, estimating distances and calculating strategies. There was no movement whatsoever around the buildings— strange. Earlier, there had been guards, people moving about, vehicles arriving and departing. Yet there must be people there. Smoke issued from two chimneys in the house and one in the small building beside the nearby barn.

The strike last night had put them on the alert. Bolan estimated the distances once more. The road out of the complex stretched away from him. There was no back way out. Any Soviet running for a vehicle would have to pass through Bolan's field of fire.

Satisfied, Bolan parked the camper closer to the farm. It was desolate and unpatrolled all around. Just the quiet world of the Idaho countryside.

Soon it was dark. He made a circuit of the area, found nothing unusual. There were no other farms within walking distance. Evidently, most of the small farmers had been bought out and had moved away when the depository was built. And with good cause. Any spill, any so-called accident here could cost the lives of anyone downwind for miles.

Bolan checked his weapons again. He laid out the ones he would be using in the morning. He filled the small combat pack with the extra Redeye rounds, some squares of C-4 plastic explosive, and a few other surprises for an emergency. Then he was ready for a five-mile run, not a jog but a run at six minutes to the mile that left him sweating and panting.

He sponged himself down with a washcloth and slid into his sleeping bag. Morning would come quickly.

4

The six attackers came out of the sky, silently, like giant deadly butterflies. They swept in from the north between fifteen and twenty feet off the ground, hugging the terrain, then swinging higher as they approached the two-story Binder Depository. Three of the ultralight aircraft, which were little more than motorized hang gliders, sailed over the depository walls at 4:30 A.M., half an hour before daylight on an autumn day in Idaho.

Each of the pilots wore protective clothing and gas masks. The first three ultralights came in formation and sprayed a heavy mixture of sulfuric acid and nausea agent 42-D across the quandrangle, at the guard post at the front of the complex and at the guard towers around the enclosure.

The second wave of three ultralights came thirty seconds later, giving the guards and outside personnel enough time to stagger from their posts. The second trio of gliders sprayed the acid-burned guards with deadly 9mm parabellum rounds from silenced Uzi submachine guns, cutting them down to a man. After this slaughter, the second group of fliers landed in the courtyard, abandoned their craft and stood guard while the first group landed in the enclosure.

Led by Aleksandr Galkin, the six men quickly swept the guard posts and, still wearing protective clothing and gas masks, killed the last two men who were trying to escape to the communications center.

Aleksandr and another man charged into the first floor of the building and found the communications room where they had expected it would be.

An Army corporal with an armband reached for his .45 but took three rounds from the silenced Uzi before he could clear iron from the polished Army holster. The second man in the room held up his hands and spread out on the floor when he was told to.

So far eighty-two seconds had elapsed from the instant the ultralights first swept over the two-story structure.

Sergei Vinogradov and two men surged past an unlocked door into the southwest corner of the quad, surprising and killing two guards. The three invaders entered the electrical power switching room. At once Sergei shut down power on the lower six floors, trapping the personnel there and deactivating any self-destruct mechanisms that were electrically triggered.

Power to the first three subfloors blinked on and off six times, and Aleksandr checked the panel. Before he could activate the controls, a woman soldier burst into the room with a .45 in her hand. He shot her in the chest and she pivoted out the doorway into the hall. Aleksandr moved to the door and made sure she was dead.

Twenty feet down the corridor a corporal reached

for his shoulder holster hardware. Six Uzi messengers drilled across his chest. A second lieutenant came around the corner of the hall from the other way, .45 already in hand. He blasted one shot at Aleksandr before he died with three rounds in his mouth.

Aleksandr ran to the communications board. It was as he had been told: simple to operate. He stripped off his protective clothing and boots. Then he studied the complex for a moment, flicked on the master switch and picked up the microphone.

"To all personnel in the complex. Cease firing! There shall be no more armed opposition, or everyone in the depository will die! I am in control of the electrical switching plant. All electrical power has been shut down for the lower six levels. You are now my prisoners. My men control all topside areas. You are held as hostages in the ten levels below ground. If there is any more resistance above ground, the levels will be destroyed one by one. Everyone above ground must move out to the front of the quad. My automatic weapons will be covering you.

"To all personnel in the lower levels. Your lives are in the palm of my hand. If you wish to live, do exactly—I repeat, *do exactly*—as you are told.

"First. Lie down. Do not use any hand weapons or manual destruct systems. I am aware of the six types of destruct devices here. I have activated none of these systems. You are now totally helpless. No one else will be killed if you do exactly as you are told.

"The central safety stairway has been electronically locked at each level. I repeat: the safety stairway has been electronically locked at each level. Your officer's keys will not open the stairwell doors.''

As Aleksandr spoke, his men were busy. According to plan, Sergei remained barricaded in the electric switching center. Having removed their protective gear, two men worked room by room through the two floors above ground, disarming everyone they encountered. There was little opposition once it was announced on the loudspeaker that the entire underground staff was being held hostage.

The two others swept the first level, picking up all weapons, locking all personnel in two equipment rooms where they would be harmless.

The same team picked up a third and descended to the second level. They were met at the door with machine-gun fire. Immediately they reported the incident to Aleksandr in the control center.

A moment later there was a rolling rumble deep below, and the ground shook briefly. Then the speakers came on in all ten levels, plus the two floors above ground and all external speakers.

''To all you heroes on the second level. Your attack on my men just resulted in the total destruction of level ten. Fourteen men and women were on duty there. They and the special devices and cultures in those areas are now destroyed. If you wish to risk the lives of those on level nine, continue your resistance. If you wish to cooperate, get on your phone and talk to me. You have sixty seconds to make up your mind, starting now.''

Within ten seconds the phone rang on Aleksandr's

communications panel. There would be no more resistance on level two.

The attackers swept onto that level and executed the highest-ranking man on the floor, a first lieutenant with numerous decorations on his shirt. They shot him six times in the heart, rounded up the other personnel, locked them in a closet, then hurried down to the next level.

There was no opposition on level three. They worked their game plan and moved to level four. At first it seemed there would be no opposition there, either. Aleksandr had left the commo board and moved to meet his team on the fourth level underground.

Staff Sergeant Napoleon "Leon" Fetterson hid behind a filing cabinet as the other workers on S-4 assembled on orders. Sergeant Fetterson had put in two tours in Nam and been a POW; he knew what an enemy could do, especially one clever enough to break into the depository. Any of these goods in the wrong hands could bring instant death to thousands of people. There was no possibility that he was going to be a prisoner again.... No way. He gripped his M-16.

He waited until the attackers locked his friends in the decontamination room. They'd be safe there. Just one bottle of this nerve gas could kill an entire city.

Sergeant Fetterson flicked the selector switch of his M-16 to automatic fire. The enemy wore strange uniforms, light green but not camouflage suits. Not decontam rigs, either. For just a moment when he looked at them he saw small men with Oriental faces screaming at him, slapping him around, kicking him just to see him cry out. He would never be a prisoner again, not of anyone! Sergeant Fetterson stepped from behind the cabinet, straightened and fired a burst of five rounds into the attacking force, then another burst and another until the magazine went dry.

Two of the men folded up and slammed against the wall. One returned a quick burst from a soundless weapon, but no shots hit Sergeant Fetterson. He turned his weapon at the last enemy, forgetting that he was out of ammunition. The third man threw up his hands in surrender. Sergeant Fetterson moved forward slowly, his finger still on the trigger. He had almost retrieved one of the dropped weapons, an Uzi submachine gun, when the door in front of him jolted open and another green-clad man stormed in.

Sergeant Fetterson saw only the short black weapon bucking in the man's hand. Then lead began pummeling him, jolting the empty weapon from his hand, crawling up his torso, setting his blood on fire. He saw one slug coming at his face. He watched it with fascination, felt it sting his forehead, then penetrate his skin and his skull and blast into his frontal lobes, mashing them into pulp and ripping the last traces of consciousness and life from his body.

"Where the hell did he come from?" Aleksandr screamed at the one remaining upright man. The guy shook his head, started to speak but couldn't.

"The canisters! Get them to the elevator! Quickly, man, no time left."

Aleksandr glanced at his two men on the floor. One was dead. The other would be dead in an hour.

"Come on, move!"

Aleksandr ran down the cement corridor, looking into rooms. Halfway down he found what he wanted. The room's double doors were marked: PD69 CC-HA-DXY-198.

Aleksandr opened one door and stared at the sudden-death containers inside. They were cylinders eighteen inches in diameter and six feet long. Each rested on a concrete cocoon twice that size. There were two tiers of canisters. Each concrete cradle had spaces for lift-truck loading bars to slide in and pick up the deadly poison gas canister.

Aleksandr opened the other door and waved the forklift truck inside. "Go, dammit! Go!"

It took almost ten minutes to get the first three canisters into the large elevator that served all levels. Though the power had been left on for the elevator, it would work only on levels four through one.

The elevator unloaded at a dummy shack outside the quadrangle and adjacent to a helicopter-landing pad. Truth to tell, Aleksandr had not been sure where the elevator would surface.

They unloaded the canisters onto a concrete pad and rushed back down to level four to pick up three more, all that could be contained in the elevator at one time.

When the final three canisters made it topside, the first streaks of light were filtering through the darkness in the east. Aleksandr looked at his watch. Exactly twenty minutes had elapsed since they sprayed their toxic surprise over the quad. They were on schedule.

He strode through the quad to the front door and saw fifteen people sitting on the ground in front of the flagpole. He fired a burst from his Uzi over them. He had taken the silencer off and the sudden angry sound of the machine gun brought screams of terror from the people.

"Down on your faces!" he bellowed at them. "Lie down, all of you! If anyone moves, he dies. Right now!"

Aleksandr fired another burst and watched the Americans cowering on the ground. He waved at his man standing on the roof and motioned for him to come down. They both went back to the helicopter pad.

They had three minutes. The two choppers had better arrive on time. If this was any kind of a secure installation, it would have hourly check-ins by phone or radio and codes of some kind.

He looked to the north. Nothing yet. Quickly he went over the rest of the plans. The two big choppers would settle down in exactly two minutes and three canisters would be loaded in each. Then the helicopters would take the men and vanish south, but make a large circle and head north. In three hours they would cross the unmarked and unguarded boundary between the United States and Canada. From then on it was a matter simply of shipping industrial chemicals.

He sent the roof guard to get Sergei.

Aleksandr suddenly saw two helicopters with no markings of any kind swinging along the contours of the ground. They lifted slightly to clear the wires, then settled down side by side near the chopper pad just outside the compound. He was surprised how large they were, but the weight of the canisters required them to be that size. He didn't know what kind these helicopters were; that had been left to the air experts.

In ten minutes all three canisters were loaded and tied down securely. Aleksandr spoke to the man who had stood guard on the roof. The man was an American, the last one he had hired.

"We won't be needing you anymore, Lewis," Aleksandr said.

"But you told me it would be for a month, a job for a month at a thousand a week."

"Looks like something is wrong with that weapon," Aleksandr said. He reached for the Uzi, and Lewis handed it to him. The leader checked the bolt, found a round in the chamber and shrugged. Aleksandr lifted the muzzle of the short weapon and sent five rounds into Lewis's chest.

The mercenary died before he knew he was hurt. He jolted backward from the force of the rounds and sprawled on the concrete with only a touch of a frown on his young face.

Aleksandr stepped through the open door of the chopper. He made sure Sergei and his last man were on board his helicopter, then without a backward glance at the dead man, gave a thumbs-up motion with his hand and the birds lifted off.

5

Mack Bolan heard helicopters. Then they came into view, two of them, low, hedgehopping, never more than thirty or forty feet off the green valley floor. Both had twin rotors, and as far as he could see neither had any markings. Not even NC civilian markings.

They were headed north and moving at top speed. They were soon out of sight.

He had just moved into position above the dairy farmhouse. It seemed the same as on the previous afternoon. No cars were visible. One of the doors of the big barn was partially open. No one walked guard at the gate, but the two dogs still prowled.

A screen door slammed at the rear of the structure. It was just after 5:00 A.M., and the dawn had arrived a mere five minutes earlier, giving the choppers and the small hills a bright, electric look.

Bolan lay in the grass for one last look at the target, then loaded an HE round, sat up and braced his feet on the ground in front of him. He boosted the Redeye to his shoulder, set the range and zeroed in on the front door of the farmhouse.

The round went off with much the same sound and feel of the old 3.5 bazookas, an intense swooshing.

Equal amounts of force were expelled out both ends of the tube, blasting a rolling pall of smoke and dust behind him and slamming the Redeye high-explosive missile forward. There was no need for a test round. The first shot went through the top of the gate and exploded against the front door of the house, lifting the second floor inches above its support and leaving the front of the house sagging.

Bolan was on his feet at once, the big weapon abandoned. His M-16 on automatic, he charged down the hill, running now, the Sixteen on his hip chattering off 3-round bursts of assault fire as he went.

He slammed the second magazine in as he approached the gate, which had been blown off its hinges. He charged through the blasted door into the still-smoking living room. The body of a man was sprawled over a plush chair opposite the door. His left arm had been blown off at his shoulder, and the side of his head was shredded with hot metal. A TV set gaped at the Executioner with the picture tube and protective glass front both shattered inward.

A groan came from the next room and Bolan charged down the hall to the door. Cautiously he entered, the M-16 leading, and saw a man on a single bed, his arm gashed and bleeding. The wounded man had no weapon.

"Where are the others?" Bolan barked.

Frightened eyes looked up. "Gone." He was a kid, no more than eighteen. His eyes pleaded. "Can you stop the blood?"

Bolan darted back to the hall, went through the rest of the rooms, one by one working up to the second floor. There was no one else in the house. The blast would have drawn anyone from the other buildings.

Bolan returned to the boy in the bedroom, opening a first-aid pouch on his web belt. He disinfected the long gash, then wrapped it tightly to stop the bleeding.

As he worked, he questioned the survivor.

"Where did the others go?"

"I'm not sure. They all flew out of here about four-fifteen. Some of them weren't very good on those ultralights."

"You know about those things?"

"Yeah. That's my specialty. I taught two of those guys to fly. They wouldn't tell me where they were going. But I heard one of them say something to the others about Binder. Why would they go to the chemical plant?"

The black-clad warrior checked his watch. It was five-twenty.

"Did they have weapons?"

"Yeah. Short, stubby little things with silencers on them. And they had special tanks on the planes with pressure bottles and some chemicals. I saw them practicing with them once."

"Is there a car here that runs?"

"My bike's outside. A Honda 450."

"Stay here. I'll be back. Don't destroy any scrap of paper, anything. What was your job here after they left?"

"Told me to clean up the place, gather everything together and burn it."

"They weren't coming back?"

"No."

"Wait here."

Bolan grabbed the keys to the motorcycle. Outside he stripped off his weapons and webbing and pushed them under some wreckage from the house. He jumped on the cycle and gunned down the lane. Once you have ridden a motorcycle, you never forget how.

He took the corner into the wider gravel road and a mile later was on the blacktop road leading to the Binder facility. More like Hellbinder, he thought to himself.

Once, not so long ago, a Chinese secret agent in New York had said to Bolan, "You remind me of a highbinder. Do you know that term? A highbinder was a hatchet man for the tongs. He killed people with a hatchet. When there was trouble in Chinatown," the guy had chuckled, "they sent for the highbinder to ax the problem."

Mack had set the man straight. "I'm nobody's paid assassin," he'd said. "The people you're talking about were enforcers, killing people who refused protection. I kill for justice."

"Then we have another name that describes your life, if not your work," grinned the Chinese spook. "You live in a world we call a hellbinder—a world that is being attacked from every direction at once!"

True, Bolan had thought. And the name came back to him now, an echo of the name of the chemical plant. The Binder facility would unleash the stormy conditions of a hellbinder for sure. . . .

Before Bolan reached the place, he heard sirens. At first he thought they were fire trucks, then he saw they were ambulances, coming from the opposite direction, from Emmett.

When he arrived at the chemical plant there was a cordon of uniformed military around the entrance. No one was being admitted. The men were grim, the weapons loaded.

"Move on!" a furious second lieutenant snapped at Bolan.

The Executioner brought the motorcycle parallel to the soldier and grabbed his arm with a grip that would not be shaken off. The young officer gazed wide-eyed at him. Bolan growled. "I've got family working in there. What are those helicopters landing for?"

"There were some military people hurt! That's all I can say.... Move along, or I'll put you under military arrest," the officer blustered.

Bolan looked up as the whup-whup-whup of four large Army choppers came down from the sky. The choppers vanished, landing behind the two-story building. They were CH-47 Chinooks, Bolan noted, big, double-rotor birds that could haul forty-four combat troops ready for war.

The nightfighter rode slowly past the building, then made a U-turn on the blacktop roadway and came back. He saw a squad of eight soldiers wearing fatigues jogging around the corner of the quad, all combat ready with M-16s at high port.

He watched as the troopers replaced the class-B uniformed men and women on the front line. A sergeant pushed back his steel helmet and quickly ordered twenty-four men into position across the twin driveways of the chemical plant.

The Executioner spun the wheel on the Honda and roared back toward the Soviet spy headquarters.

Within the hour Bolan and the wounded man, who said that his name was Paul, took the house apart. All they found were some scraps of paper with Spanish writing on them and one or two notes in English. One of them mentioned San Salvador.

The dead man in the living room had been with the group since Paul joined them two weeks before. He and Paul were to have finished cleaning up here, and the older man was meant to join the others. Paul was to have been paid off and put up in town. It wasn't clear where the other man was to have gone.

Bolan looked at the dead man on the floor again. He must have been a KGB enforcer. His pockets revealed a great deal. He had a driver's license in the name of Georgi Smith. The wallet also contained an address in Vancouver, British Columbia, six hundred dollars and an airline ticket from Boise to Vancouver.

The Executioner looked at the evidence and knew they were ahead of him. The San Salvador connection rankled. What exactly had this Russian taken from the depository? He needed more information.

Paul had already filled him in on names. One of the leaders was Aleksandr Galkin, and the second in charge was a Sergei something.

"Are we going to call the sheriff?" Paul asked. "We can't just leave this body lying here."

Bolan knew what to do next, not through any rational process but by instinct, a deep sense a man develops in combat necessary for survival.

The warrior explained to Paul what he had become involved in. Then he tapped the body on the floor.

"Was he helping you in the cleanup?"

"No. He just gave the orders."

"And once you had the place clean of any leads, he would have killed you and ridden your bike to Boise."

"Killed me? You're kidding!" Paul eyed the dead man. "He was kind of a friend. His English wasn't very good, but he didn't push me around."

"He was KGB. An enforcer. A hired killer. He'd shoot you dead and eat lunch off your chest before your body had cooled."

Paul shook his head, disbelieving.

"Believe it, kid. Now take whatever is yours, then ride your bike out of here and forget you ever came."

Bolan took some cash from the dead man's wallet. He handed it to Paul. "Here are your wages. Now beat it."

The Executioner watched the kid ride down the lane, toward the blacktop road and disappear. Then he took the scraps of paper and the Vancouver address, picked up his M-16 and jogged up the hill.

Half an hour later he had the Redeye hidden in the compartment of the camper and was headed for Emmett. By now there would be plenty of talk in town about what had happened at the chemical plant.

Bolan found a phone booth, used his Calling Card number and dialed the Stony Man Farm complex where he could never go again. An unfamiliar voice answered. Bolan asked if the Bear was there. A moment later the familiar growl assured Bolan he had the right man.

"This is your far West correspondent," Bolan said. "What the hell happened to the chemical industry?"

"Plenty. Even after the warning, they got clobbered and stripped. Six guys, six ultralight aircraft and two big choppers. Don't know who, but they knew what they wanted. They took out only one item, PD69CC-HA-DXY-198. They took six six-foot canisters. Each one weighs almost two thousand pounds. That's a recently developed duplex nerve gas."

"A bad one, Bear?"

"A superbad one. A liquified gas, highly compressed. When it's released into the atmosphere, the droplets explode into a ten-thousand-to-one volume of gas. It descends as a killer fog, heavier than air. It attacks the central nervous system of all vertebrates, and brings a quick death—but agonizing—in ten to fifteen seconds. There is no antidote, even if there were time to effect a cure."

"I was near the place just now."

"What in hell is going on, West Coast?"

"I'd say Canada for transshipment and El Salvador for end use. Just a guess."

"Better than anything *we* have. I'll keep you out of this as usual. You flying away?"

"Soon as I can come up with a piece of paper."

"Ordinarily...."

"Hey, forget it. Things are different now. Thanks, Bear. I'm moving."

Bolan hung up, got in the camper and drove. His first stop was a parking garage in Boise, the biggest one in town. He figured the camper might be there for a while. Before he left, he packed a suitcase with enough clothes to make him look like a tourist and, regrettably, laid aside all his weapons. Customs.

He undid the bottom seam of a sport coat and carefully inserted twenty one-hundred-dollar bills in each side near the back. The money made the jacket hang nicely, and a few extra dollars would always help.

At a bank he bought four thousand dollars' worth of American Express traveler's checks, then caught a cab for the airport. Another five thousand in cash, from an earlier profitable venture, was in one of the two wallets he carried.

At a magazine stand he bought the *New York Times* and two newsmagazines, wanting as much information as he could get about El Salvador, Honduras, Nicaragua and the whole mess in Central America.

The first leg of his trip took him to San Francisco, where he had access to some people who could help him with his "paper" problem.

The paper he needed was a false U.S. passport and the backup identification to help him in and out of the country.

6

It was dark when he landed in San Salvador. A taxi took Bolan into the downtown area where he went to a good hotel, but not the best. The room was small, the bed lumpy, but he slept. He had gained an hour in time, since the longitude at El Salvador is nearly the same as Chicago's.

Bolan woke at 5:30 A.M., as usual. He thought he heard someone outside his door, but when he unlocked it and moved the chair, he found the hallway empty.

He breakfasted in the dining room, then returned to his room and changed into a pair of blue jeans, a blue T-shirt with *California* written on it and a denim jacket several shades darker than the pants. It was to be his mercenary uniform.

He asked the English-speaking desk clerk if he could help find someone. All he had was a name. The clerk consulted a telephone directory and gave him an address.

"This man, he is not with the best reputation."

"I don't plan on marrying him, just some business."

"He is, what do you say, a shady character. Not above making the robbery of a tourist."

"Thanks, pardner. I'll be careful." He paused. "I guess it's against the law to carry a gun here, right?"

"Very right, sir. You will be shot at once if caught with a firearm of any type. Very much against the law."

"I was afraid of that. Thanks again."

Outside, Bolan took a stroll. It was easy to tell he was being followed. The small man doing the work was not the best—he was too obvious; this suggested there would be a second tail who would be more discreet and stick to Bolan once he lost the first one.

The Executioner ditched the first tail in a market by doubling back, then watched from a small café while the small man searched and at last gave up and backtracked toward the hotel. It took Bolan ten minutes to spot the second tail. He was thin and tall, wearing washed whites and a straw hat pulled low over his face.

The warrior left the restaurant and walked directly toward the man. He stared him in the eye and asked if he had a match. The tail hesitated, then shook his head and said in Spanish that he did not speak English. He turned and with only a quick backward glance walked away. When he was out of sight Bolan ran in the opposite direction for two blocks, caught a taxi and gave the driver the slip of paper with the address.

People were everywhere. It was hard to tell a civil war had been going on for five years. Five million people were packed into a nation about the size of

Massachusetts, at about the same density, and most were jammed in along the coast.

The cab driver took him down the main thoroughfare, along a narrow winding street into a wide avenue of luxurious homes and then, turning a corner, to a fine house with an iron gate and bell at the sidewalk. He took his payment and left, and Bolan rang the bell. A panel opened in a door twenty feet away, and momentarily a large muscular black man emerged from another door at the side. He wore a tight T-shirt, white pants and a colorful sash around his waist. He stood beyond the gate looking at Bolan. He spoke in English.

"Morning, man. You're a long way from Pismo Beach."

The Executioner laughed. "And you're one hell of a long shot from it, too. What you doing down here?"

"Maybe the same thing you are. Who you looking for?"

"Gentleman by the handle of Diego Fortuna. Know him?"

"Could be. Why are you here? What do you want?"

"Hey, lighten up. A man told me I could find work with Fortuna, and since I don't have any war going at the moment, I thought I'd test the wage scale."

"You got any references?"

"A few bullet holes. Do they count?"

"I think I can let you in the gate," muttered the big man. "Diego will want to see you." He opened the gate, closed it and stood in front of Bolan. Suddenly he pushed the Executioner in the chest with an open hand.

Quick as a striking cobra, Bolan trapped the spread hand on his chest with his right arm, grabbed the man's elbow with his left hand, pressed it upward and prepared to snap the arm like a dried twig.

"Okay!" the black man yelled.

The Executioner let up on the pressure, and the other man stretched his fingers, working them to be sure they weren't injured.

"You're a good soldier," Bolan said. "But so am I."

"They call me Blackie," the big man grunted. "Never could figure the hell why." He grinned. "Come on in and say howdy, Brooklyn style."

In El Salvador, as with most of Central America, a small percentage of the population is extremely rich, an equally small number of people are middle class, and millions live at the poverty and starvation level. Diego Fortuna was one of the nouveau riche. The house was indeed luxurious, with fine furniture, brass fixtures, rich hand-carved wooden ornamentation and oil paintings bathed in the perfect illumination of small lamps. The hall and rooms that Bolan saw were carpeted, some with Persian rugs spread over the carpet.

They passed through a hall to a study lined with glass-enclosed book cabinets. There was a large globe in one corner and a big business-style desk of dark cherry with a gleaming top in the middle of the room. Only a phone and one file folder lay on top of the desk.

Behind it sat a man with dark hair, a full, closely clipped beard and darting brown eyes. He remained seated as the two men entered.

Diego Fortuna addressed Blackie. "Your preliminary evaluation?"

"I wouldn't want to go up against him. He used a hand press on me that was about to break my fingers off. I'd say he's a real find."

Diego nodded and Blackie left the room with a wink at Bolan, who stood just inside the doorway.

"How did you get my name?" Fortuna asked.

"From a friend in the States. He said not to tell you who he was."

"That in itself tells me." Diego smiled. When he stood, Bolan saw that he was barely five feet tall. He wore a business suit with a vest and a silk tie worth thirty dollars.

"You heard there may be employment here, but you don't know the employer or the mission, right?"

"Whatever it is, I can handle it. I'm plenty experienced."

"Yes, I would expect that you are." Diego moved to the front of the desk and leaned back against it. "Do you have any qualms about combat situations?"

"That's what I specialize in."

"Maybe you're overqualified for the position."

"I was a headhunter in Nam. Do you know what that means?"

Diego stared back at Bolan without answering. Then he said, "The pay is five hundred American dollars a week in any combat situation. If there is no combat, the pay is two hundred a week. Satisfactory?"

"Fine."

"This operation will last a week, maybe more. The timing isn't specific yet. We can contact you at your hotel, the Plantation?"

"Call me," Bolan said. "The name's Mack Scott." He turned and walked out of the room.

The lone warrior strode to the street and waved down a cab.

7

The Executioner believed the best way to kill time was to work it to death, but now that solution was denied him. He had to occupy himself with the same things mercenaries usually do: wine, women and song.

He gave the driver the name of his hotel. Bolan knew he could not be sure if he had arrived before the canisters from Vancouver. He couldn't even be certain that the canisters of deadly gas would be delivered here. But it was logical and it was the only choice he had. He would play out the logic string.

As he rolled back to the hotel, Bolan knew his transition from hired gun for the U.S. to independent warrior was complete. True, he used Kurtzman as a source, but he would always have to use all the sources he could tap.

He was strictly playing a lone hand, with police agencies in several areas hunting for him again. He was wanted by the CIA and several other intelligence agencies, and the KGB had an extensive file on him under his various names.

Mack Bolan knew he was not a superman, not a special individual with special privileges. He came from common lower-middle-class stock. He had worked hard all his life and he was dedicated to the proposition that someone had to fight on the side of right no matter what the costs or casualties. That was simply what he did. And he did it well.

Bolan loved his country. He had fought and almost died in the nation's military uniform, and he still felt a surge of emotion when the "Star Spangled Banner" played or when the flag passed in a parade.

He had come out of Vietnam after two tours of duty to go home on emergency leave. A tragedy in his family had pointed him dead center at the Mafia, and he began his holy war against the most unholy of the time.

The Mafia had been his first war, as he pounded, bombed, shot and tore up two dozen Mafia families, riddling the ranks, avenging one-hundredfold his own kin. He had challenged their force with an equal amount of his own and blasted them back into the sewers they had originally crawled from.

His second war had been against terrorism. He had worked closely with the federal government, striking at terrorists who threatened the U.S. and its allies. Again he was fighting fire with fire, bombs with bombs, and as Colonel John Phoenix he made them pay dearly, wiping out whole nests of agents and terrorists. But they kept coming on.

That war came to an end for him with the attack on Stony Man Farm and the aftermath of the Russian deception. The KGB had set up a popular pro-Western labor leader in Europe and assassinated him, making it look as if Colonel John Phoenix had done the task in front of thousands of witnesses; with plastic surgery the KGB had transformed a convict from a Russian prison into a copy of Colonel Phoenix, then had him kill the labor leader.

Bolan spent months in Russia's underground searching for the man who had set up the deception, and at last took a swath out of the KGB management in a deadly maneuver. But then, when in front of the President of the United States in the Oval Office he killed the mole who had betrayed Stony Man Farm, Bolan cut his chances of reestablishing ties with the U.S. government.

And now he was out on his own again, answering to no man, driven by his need to avenge the murder of his lover and friend, April Rose, and driven too by the nature of his calling, which was to kill unmercifully so that the good and the gentle could survive; in its way, such killing was altogether merciful.

Bolan used secret documents he brought back from Russia to find and destroy as many KGB operatives and operations as he could.

It was kill or be killed, and Mack Bolan was ready.

The enemy had been warned. He was coming at them in every way and with every weapon and power he could command until they were all dead and buried—or until Mack Bolan had drawn his last breath and said goodbye to life after a rugged fight.

He would still be fighting when the KGB carried his head on a gold platter up to 2 Dzerzhinsky Square for the celebration. His eyes would still be accusing them.

Bolan realized the taxi had stopped in front of the

hotel. He paid the driver five *colones* and went into the hotel.

He nodded at the clerk, bought one English and one Spanish newspaper off the stand, then strolled past the clerk.

"Diego did not laugh when I told him your remark," Bolan said as he walked.

"Surely you did not..." the clerk began, keeping up with him.

The big man with the steely blue eyes laughed and shook his head. "I did not, but next time I see him, maybe I will. It would be tactful of you to keep me informed of any more spies that the great one sends to watch me."

The clerk leaned closer to Bolan.

"One man went through your room while you were gone," he said. "Another man, the one behind the newspaper, is watching you and will follow you."

Bolan thanked the clerk and walked on to the man with the paper. He was dressed in a lightweight white suit and tie. The Executioner sat beside the slender man on the wide sofa.

"Hi, pal. No reason to make this hard for you. I feel the need of a drink. Come into the bar and share one with me."

The man shook his head. Bolan took the guy by the arm, his big hand viselike around the darker man's biceps, and lifted him from the sofa.

"Let's have that friendly drink. You do speak English?"

"No inglés."

"I bet." Bolan switched to his adequate Spanish as he guided the man into the bar. "I won't say a word about this to Señor Fortuna," Bolan said.

At that the man nodded and thanked Bolan. They sat down at the bar and ordered local beer. The man said his name was Pepe and said little else.

"I suppose you've been through my room by now." Bolan glared at him. Pepe held up his hands, protesting his innocence. Bolan softened. "You can tell Diego," he said, smiling, "that I'm exactly what I said I was. I kill people. I fight on any side if the price is right. Now that we have that straight, where is the best whorehouse in town?"

Pepe smiled for the first time. Bolan knew he had struck a responsive chord.

Pepe gave him the address, and Bolan finished the beer, bought the Salvadoran another and then went up to his room.

Whoever searched it had been good at his work. Bolan would not have known except for the way the newspaper was left on top of his suitcase. Bolan had placed it so the corners touched the edge of the suitcase, forming an exact equilateral triangle. Now the triangle was not perfect.

He removed his jacket and dropped on the bed. He went through the English newspaper from Miami, then the Spanish one, but found little of interest. He had an early lunch in the dining room, again inviting Pepe to eat with him. When Bolan checked the desk on the way to his room, he found a familiar face.

"Blackie, you no-good honky lover, what you doing here?"

"Got two tickets to the big game. Soccer, man! Bootball, Central American style. Big playoff game in the stadium. Want to go?"

They went. It gave Bolan a chance to pump Blackie, who didn't mind talking.

"Hell, man, Diego gave me the tickets and said to take you. He don't want you getting in trouble in some cathouse and winding up in jail just when we pull out. Looks like it'll be tomorrow sometime."

The soccer was good, although it was a cut below European.

"You been out on these runs before for Diego?" Bolan asked casually.

"Hell, yes! I'm the pointman. And I think he wants you to ride with me. We go ahead of the main party in an old jeep. We try to draw any hostile fire. Hell, I'm telling you how to be a pointman?"

"You lasted this long?" Bolan asked.

"Shit, nobody can kill me. I been on six runs now in the point. That's why I get a thousand a run. Got cut up bad once, but nothing fatal. I figure about five more trips and I can go back to Detroit and open a little ribs place. Damn, I love ribs."

"This one going down fast?"

"Tomorrow."

"What's the mission?"

"Probably the usual. We filter out of town and meet in the boonies. When we're far enough out, we form up into a small convoy, pull out the weapons and charge up into the hills. The Sierra Madre range is back there. First we have to get through the coast range, which ain't as high. Heard something about a truck we'll be taking in. But just where we're going we never know. Usually we hook up with a guide who takes us to one of the guerrilla camps. The central-government forces never get back in the hills too far. Afraid of getting their damned heads blown off.''

He laughed then and turned to watch the game. One of the home team forwards missed an easy shot.

"Ain't a matter of whether or not we're gonna get shot up. It's when and where and how bad."

"And we'll be the bait?"

"True."

The home team won the soccer game. The pair of Americans left and had dinner at a restaurant Blackie knew, and afterward went to the hotel. Blackie made a call from the lobby as the Executioner waited. The big black man returned, grinning.

"Okay, my man. It's on, it's a go! I'll pick you up in the morning at 6:15. Pack and leave all your traveling gear here. We take a taxi out, transfer to a bus and then meet our group about ten miles farther on into the foothills. Nice country. Sleep good, man, we're going to need it all tomorrow!''

8

Ambassador A. Ellington Johnson, up as usual a little after nine o'clock, went through his fifteen-minute regimen of flexibility exercises. On schedule, his aide briefed him regarding new material from the news wire, special signals from Washington, and the latest guerrilla situation. The Communist-led rebels had been making increasingly bold moves lately, some even in the city of San Salvador.

Johnson sat on the edge of the Mancisor intermediate-level home-gym exercising machine. He shipped it everywhere he went. As a medical doctor he knew that he had to take care of the body as well as the soul. It was the dedication, the day-by-day mental push to do it, that was tough.

Johnson hadn't really wanted this job with the administration. His medical practice in Washington, D.C., put him in touch with the administration, and his contributions over the years to the Republican party had now been "rewarded." The fact that he spoke Spanish like a native and had spent two years in Mexico City as an intern helped. He at last agreed to a four-year stint, but no more.

At fifty-five, he was too old to play the diplomatic game, but he was locked into it now, and he went at the contest with fierce determination.

The ambassador listened as his aide droned on about the international situation, knowing that he should be on top of everything. He did ten minutes of hard pumping on the stationary bicycle and retreated to the shower.

"Mr. Ambassador," his aide called after him. "Don't forget that you have that ten-thirty meeting with a contact who is going to help set up a session with Jose Morales. Señor Morales thinks he can work out a face-to-face with the guerrillas."

"Yes, yes, I'll be there."

Johnson relaxed in the shower. This week, the water was hot. Next week, who knew? He let the hot water pour over him and tried to forget all the complications in this job he really never wanted. Martha would rather not have come down here, either, but they both had. Ronnie had talked them into it.

An hour later the big Lincoln Continental stopped near the outskirts of the city. It was on a little-used road behind some squalid, delapidated shacks. His aide said the lowest economic class lived here. The people were undoubtedly in the worst health, as well. Johnson sighed. He had been able to find absolutely no time to deal with the wretched situation here. There should be time for a clinic, something, but no, he was shunted from meeting to conference to talk to special appearance to goddamned everything.

This Lincoln was the safe one. It had bulletproofing all the way around, glass and metal, and the engine was special. Even with the murderous amount of additional weight, the big tank would do 120 mph on an open highway. It even had a steel-plated undercarriage to protect against land mines.

The ambassador would have liked to roll down the window, but since El Salvador had been deemed a "red" zone for danger, the windows, an inch and a half thick, were sealed shut. He sat in air-conditioned comfort and listened to a tape of *The Nutcracker Suite*. It made him homesick, remembering how his daughter had been in ballet school and at last had danced in the Christmas ballet on stage.

There were three people in the car: the ambassador, the chauffeur, and the bodyguard, Willis, whom the ambassador felt wasn't needed. His aide was supposed to come along but had to cancel at the last minute.

"Where are they?" Ambassador Johnson asked the man beside him, who was checking the operation of an Israeli-made Uzi submachine gun. It looked an evil killing device. As a medical man, the ambassador understood what those deadly slugs could do to a human body.

"They're twenty minutes late," Willis said, shifting on the seat. "Think I'll get out and see what's going on."

"Maybe we should just drive on. This isn't the best neighborhood."

Willis frowned, twisting his mouth to one side the way he usually did. "Probably. But let me take a quick recon. I'll be right back."

Willis tapped the glass separating the front from

the rear and twisted his hand as if unlocking something. At once the door lock beside him popped up.

"Be right back," Willis said, unlatching and opening the door. As he stood, the side of his face burst in a shower of blood and bone fragments as a 9mm parabellum smashed into his cheek and exited through his nose. The force of the round pushed him against the top of the limousine.

Quickly, as though one explosion, six more deadly lead messengers slammed into Willis, two through his chest, one through his left eye, one into his stomach. He sagged against the open door, then slumped half into and half out of the car.

"Move it! Move it!" Dr. Johnson shouted. The engine ground and the big car surged ahead. Willis's body was caught between the wildly swinging heavy door and the seat. As the car careened down the hard-packed earth path, Willis fell to the ground and rolled away.

No more rounds came at the big car. But twenty feet down the roadway, a shoulder-held rocket launcher fired. The Russian-made missile flew fifty feet from a tumbled-in shack, hit the Lincoln's left front wheel and exploded, destroying the tire and flipping the heavy car onto its side. The driver's head slammed violently against the thick glass and split open like an overripe melon; the dead driver fell heavily to the passenger's side of the limo. The four wheels spun in the air as the big car rocked once more and remained on its side.

In the back, Ambassador Johnson, who had been sitting on the right-hand side, now hung awkwardly, still pinned to the seat, still wearing his seat belt. The explosion had slammed him against the padded rear cushion, but he was alive and fully conscious.

The guerrillas would be nearby. But how could he escape? Was the far door still unlocked?

He heard voices outside. Shouts in Spanish. He couldn't understand all they were saying, but he got enough of it. They would tip the heavy rig back upright, then get out the "criminal diplomat" from America. The hated one would be in their hands and they would torture him and see how much pain he could stand before they executed him slowly. It would be a great victory for the Farabundo Marti Liberación Nacional. Long live the liberation!

Moments later a stern, sharp voice shouted instructions that the ambassador couldn't make out. At once someone bounded to the top side of the car and tried the door, which opened upward with much tugging and pulling. A face looked inside. The mouth was thin, eyes narrowly set and dark. The man wore a soft green fatigue cap common among guerrillas.

"Pardon our abrupt halting of your vehicle, Mr. Ambassador, but we wish to speak with you, and this seemed the only way. You will kindly unfasten your seat belt so we can assist you from the limousine."

The man spoke in perfect English. Dr. Johnson answered him in perfect colloquial Spanish.

"I will be pleased to do that. May I have your name and the name of whoever you are representing?"

"That won't be necessary. Names are of no real importance. Please, we'll help you out."

A few moments later he stepped on the side of the jump seat and was lifted out the door, then helped to the ground.

The spokesman was a thin man with a black mustache and penetrating eyes. He pushed the fatigue cap back slightly and nodded.

"Mr. Ambassador, we have heard that you are an honorable man, a good man. We have heard that you speak our language, understand our problems and want to help us to make our nation whole again. We hope all this is true. Come, we have a long trip."

"I'm a prisoner, then?"

"You are our honored guest for the next few days while we talk with others of your nation."

Johnson looked at the leader and frowned. "How long have you had that wound on your arm?" the ambassador asked. "It needs medical attention. My medical bag is in the front seat."

The leader nodded and a man jumped to the car to find the bag. He returned with it. One of the black handles had been blown off and there was a gash in the side, but otherwise it was intact.

"Come here and take that filthy bandage off," Johnson said, feeling secure in his medical authority.

"We have to be moving. You can treat it where we must stay tonight as the search for you begins. We will not inform the embassy until tomorrow that you are our guest. We apologize to your lady, who will worry, but we must protect ourselves."

An ancient produce truck wheezed into sight and

stopped nearby. Six men jumped on board and reached down to aid Dr. Johnson and the leader into the truck. Then the large doors were closed and the truck began rolling.

A battery powered lantern came on, breaking up the nearly total darkness inside the truck.

"Now I will treat you, Captain," Ambassador Dr. Johnson said. "If you aren't a captain, I just promoted you. If you are a general, my apologies. Now let's look at that arm."

There were some murmurs of approval that he had spoken in Spanish. The men clustered around in the bouncing truck to watch.

When the dirty bandage came off, Johnson saw a bullet wound, the lead buried half an inch into the arm.

"You're lucky it missed the bone," Dr. Johnson said. He cleaned the wound with alcohol and heard only a quick gasp as the alcohol burned a hundred raw nerve endings. "This wound is a week old. It should have started to heal better by now." He looked up. "That would have been the fight between the rebels and the government forces near the old bridge. As with any battle, it was one that nobody won."

"They know we are here. We grow stronger every day."

"I listen to Radio Venceremos, too, Captain," the doctor said. He dusted the wound with emergency sulfa, still the best survival medicine a soldier can carry that will not spoil over a long period. "You should have some antibiotics, but your pharmacy has closed. The next time you're near the embassy, stop by and I'll give you a shot of penicillin. It has to be refrigerated, or otherwise I'd have some.'' He spread Neosporin ointment over the wounds, then wrapped them with a two-inch roller bandage and taped the ends tightly.

''Good as new in two weeks if you don't get shot again. And make an appointment in two days to have that dressing changed.''

The soldiers laughed at the appointment idea.

''Thanks,'' the leader said, holding out his good right hand. ''They said you are a fine man.''

''Where are we going?''

''I can't tell you that, but as you guessed, it is out of the city and toward the north. But you already know where the FMNL strength is.''

''Do you know this man Ungo, Guillermo Ungo? I have never met him and perhaps never will. Is he an honorable man?''

''Tell him, Captain!'' one of the soldiers said. It was a tease.

The leader switched to English. ''The men make fun of me since I am only a lieutenant.'' He went back to Spanish. ''Yes, of course, I will tell you he is honorable. He is my leader—I must believe that. He also is a Marxist, which by definition I must believe is beyond reproach, above any suspicion and meriting only the highest praises.''

''And, Captain, are you a Marxist?''

''Yes, until the day I die. I believe.''

''Are all of your men?'' Dr. Johnson looked at them, staring into the eyes of each.

"Ask them," the leader said.

They were still talking when the truck stopped.

The door was opened from the outside and the soldiers rushed out, anxious to get into the open air again. Dr. Johnson pushed away their helping hands and jumped from the truck with his black bag.

They were at a coffee plantation, but not near any buildings. The truck was parked on a sharp incline and everywhere he looked, Dr. Johnson saw coffee trees. The trees extended up and down the hills in every direction.

"Where are the people who pick the coffee beans?" Dr. Johnson asked.

"In the village a mile down the road," the leader said.

"Then we must go there. As long as I can't help your nation as an ambassador, I must help the people as a doctor. Come, come, do you think I will run away? Where is this place? I will walk. You can save your petrol."

They walked.

That night Dr. Johnson fell on a mattress in a shack under a coffee tree at the edge of the village. He had talked to thirty-four patients, and had done everything from lancing a boil to informing a young wife she was pregnant.

He couldn't remember a more rewarding day since he had come to El Salvador two years ago. He lay on the pallet for only a moment, then nodded into sleep.

9

The kamikaze taxi driver delivered Bolan and Blackie well north of the capital. They waited by the side of the road for ten minutes before a bus came by. They boarded it and rode north, disembarking an hour later at a small village surrounded by coffee trees.

"Assembly point," Blackie said, dropping into his service talk. "We form up here and move out like we mean it. Should be our jeep and three or four other vehicles, all civilian, naturally. At least there'll be some firepower behind us."

They walked into the orchard of small coffee trees, most less than eight feet high, all topped and pruned for easy work around them. Some of the coffee beans were bright red, others still green.

A half mile up a dirt road they passed a sentry. Another half mile and they found the camp.

It looked more like a Sunday picnic than an army. Rebels, mercs and guerrillas would always look like lost and abandoned children, Bolan decided.

They were met by a noncommissioned officer without stripes who took them to a dour-faced little man wearing combat-green pants and a white shirt. He smiled past his drooping mustache and spoke in Spanish.

"Welcome, American. One more good man helps us a little, and a little bit helps." He tossed both men AK-47 automatic rifles. Each had a 30-round magazine, and from its weight, Bolan knew the magazine was loaded.

"Your weapon for the mission. Take care of it or you'll be charged for it. Scott," he said, using the name for Bolan given to him by Fortuna. "I am Captain Valderez. I'm in command of the convoy. You will go with Blackie in the forward jeep. You can draw three hand grenades each. Our main body will be a quarter mile behind you and there will be no connecting file. Questions?"

"Any fire control?" Bolan asked in Spanish.

"Only that you are not to fire until fired upon. We do not want to advertise that we're coming."

Blackie nodded. "Where do we pick up the fraggers?" he asked.

They were pointed toward a small two-man pup tent.

"We will move out at 1300 hours. If you haven't eaten there will be chow at 1230." The dour little man spoke more quietly. "Blackie. This is the most important one that we've been on yet."

"Hey man, we do good," Blackie said, mangling the jive talk as it came out in Spanish.

They drew their three hand grenades. Two were the old U.S. Army style, the pineapple type, the other four the newer kind, also American made, rounder and with a smooth casing. All could kill.

Lunch turned out to be beans, beef and some hard biscuits along with coffee. At 1250 hours, someone brought the jeep around and Blackie at once turned off the engine and quickly checked plugs, points, the gas supply and then the brakes. He started the engine, adjusted the air and gas mixture and when he was happy he put down the windshield and locked it in place.

"I don't want no damn glass splinters rammed up my nose when we take the first wild rounds," he said.

"Maybe we won't be hit this time," Bolan said.

Blackie laughed and picked his teeth with a knife-sharpened kitchen match. "And maybe you won't shit for a week, but the odds ain't very good. We'll get hit, the only question is how hard and how close to the mountains."

"I thought we were in the mountains," Bolan said.

"Hell, these ain't even hills. We got to get back into the tall ones, and the volcanoes. We got at least a dozen active volcanoes in this little chunk of country, you know that? Mount up, soldier. The CO just waved his magic riding crop."

Ahead, Bolan saw the small officer in charge pulling the units into line. The jeep went around two twenty-foot trucks. Each held about fifteen fully armed and combat-ready men. All had good weapons, but almost no uniforms. It looked like a ragtag outfit. But anybody can pull the trigger on an AK-47 or a machine gun. No training required. Those untrained bullets kill just as well as ones fired by a master combat veteran.

At the head of the trucks they paused. Captain

Valderez stepped up to the jeep. Now he had an MP-40 German-made submachine gun slung over his shoulder. It had what looked like a 40-round magazine in it for the 9mm parabellum rounds. He checked his watch.

"You move out in exactly one minute, Blackie. Usual precautions, and keep your speed to no more than twenty to twenty-five mph on these trails. If we get more than a half mile behind, pull up and wait for us. These trucks are in good condition, so we should be able to keep up today." The little guy tried smiling, and his white teeth gleamed. "My friends, good luck." Captain Valderez looked at his watch and waved them on.

"Watch out, adventure, here we come one more goddamned time!" Blackie said. His eyes were wide, and there was a strange smile on his face. Blackie was high on something.

"Coke, man? Blackie, you on coke?" Bolan asked him.

Blackie looked at Bolan and laughed. He goosed the accelerator, then let the speed drop back to twenty. "Hey, you do what you got to and I do what I got to."

"Is that why you do this, for the kicks? Damn hard way to make a living, Blackie."

"So far, so good. Hey, don't bitch at me until you've made a few runs down here. This ain't the usual kind of war. Anyway, who gives a damn? Two more trips and I'll have enough to start my own ribs joint back in Detroit. I got some connections back there, man. No sweat. In two years I'll be dragging in the money, profits to one hundred thousand dollars a year."

For the first ten miles the dirt road snaked through a long valley, went over a low pass and into another valley. The narrow tracks all worked upward toward the high Sierra Madre. Bolan saw coffee plantations wherever there was tillable land. The small trees marched up and down the slopes and across the valleys. He commented that there weren't as many people as he expected to see in this agricultural area. Blackie laughed.

"Shit, man, the word goes out that a convoy is going uphill, and all the natives lie low in a ditch. Too many times they been caught in the middle, and a 9mm son of a bitch doesn't care who it digs into."

The road kept rising. They paused for a moment on a small hill and saw that the other trucks were back almost a mile. The jeep idled as they waited. Both men watched the downslopes, looking for some kind of an ambush. It was not to be here.

"Christ, maybe we will get through this time," Blackie said. "No sweat! Them muthas show up, I'll blast them into Kingdom Come with my trusty forty-seven here. We got plenty of loaded magazines. I got three. You got three?"

Bolan nodded. "The convoy's closing. We can take off. We'd better keep it under twenty for a while on the hills."

"Yeah, yeah. I done it before, remember?"

They cruised along, The Executioner with the AK up, ready and set on automatic fire. They entered a stretch where the rain forest came right up to the sides of the road. There was no room for coffee trees here. Bolan tensed, expecting that this would be the type of place where an ambush might occur.

Blackie laughed. "Not yet, California. Another five miles at least before they'll hit us. Never caught us so close to the valley before."

The trucks behind closed up to a hundred yards as the road turned rough. They hit a particularly big rut and before Bolan came back down on the hard cushion, rifle and automatic fire erupted on both sides of the road. The Executioner dived headfirst out of the jeep. Blackie had slowed it to less than five miles an hour. Bolan did a front roll and tumbled sideways into the brush.

He heard the rifle slugs spanging off the jeep, saw one front tire blow out and then the jeep rise. Only then did Bolan hear the land mine explode and see the jeep tumble on its side and roll three times away from him. He slid on his belly through the dense growth away from the vehicle, then stopped and listened.

Heavier fire came from behind, where men surged from the trucks, vanishing into the jungle on both sides and moving forward in a skirmish line.

For just a moment he heard more firing ahead of him. Bolan still had the AK, and he hammered off a 5-round burst straight into the air, then rolled a dozen feet away. There was no counterfire.

He saw no sign of Blackie. The driver would be the first target, which meant Blackie probably was hit. The land mine could have caught him as well.

Now he saw shadowy forms, four or five, moving

toward him through the jungle. They wore uniforms, camouflaged green, and soft hats. They moved carefully.

Bolan lay where he was, and five minutes later a scout from his own rebel band came up near him. He gave a thumbs-up motion and pointed straight ahead. Then he pointed to his weapon. The scout nodded, and he and Bolan laid down a barrage of fire that riddled the forest.

They stopped and heard a wail of pain and sounds of retreat. By the time the rest of the detail had worked up to Bolan's position, the enemy had run. The scout moved ahead cautiously and soon was back. There was one government man dead, and one badly wounded who was now also dead. He proudly carried two M-16 U.S. military automatic rifles.

The scout brought one to Bolan, along with three full magazines.

"This one is yours, California. You earned it."

They moved out to the roadway and the scout whistled. A moment later a whistle sounded from across the road. There had been no weapons fire for ten minutes. The troops assembled on the road and looked at the jeep. Blackie lay in the road. He had taken three rifle slugs, one in his forehead and two in his chest. They dragged his body into the brush. Quick and simple. Goodbye, Blackie. Goodbye, Detroit. Goodbye, ribs place.

Captain Valderez motioned for them to move out. Bolan and the scout took the point now, jogging ahead of the trucks for two miles. Then they were replaced by two more men as they moved along the narrow forest trail at ten miles an hour.

Bolan sat in the lead vehicle with the captain.

"You have gained the respect of my men," the rebel said. "They tell me you slipped the ambush, killed one of the enemy and drove them into retreat almost singlehandedly."

"I was lucky in the ambush," Bolan said. "The rest was simply good combat work. I'll miss Blackie. He was a good man."

"Well, you will not ride the point again. Instead you will be given a command if you want one."

"Sounds interesting," Bolan said. "That means the pay would be better?"

"Much better."

Some fifteen miles up the rugged trail of a road they came to a crude roadblock. It was a guerrilla strongpoint and they passed through and were given a guide who rode in the lead rig. Bolan was taken to the last truck and put in the cab beside a dark-haired man. Bolan was not introduced to him, but there was a vague familiarity about his profile.

The man was pleasant but not talkative. He was two inches under six feet tall and about forty years old. He also was at least thirty pounds overweight. Bolan talked with the driver about the firefight, and the driver said they were lucky. It was a small band of government forces, no more than ten or twelve.

At last the third man spoke, and to Bolan's surprise it was in Russian.

"Do either of you speak Russian?" the man asked.

Bolan switched easily to his tentative Russian.

"I do somewhat, but poorly," Bolan said.

"That is wonderful! I've had no one to talk to for three days. My Spanish is bad." He held out his hand. "My name is Aleksandr Galkin."

The Executioner smiled at the KGB agent.

"So you are the big reason we are coming way up here," Bolan said. "You must have a prize package you are bringing to the rebels?"

"Yes, a special prize. One that is going to make half the world enraged and the other half joyous." He hesitated. "They say you are American, and that you routed the government forces all by yourself."

"War stories. Right now I'm a merc, I work for the highest bidder. I guess that makes me an ex-American."

Aleksandr laughed. "Then you won't be too surprised when the U.S. gets angry about my small package." He gazed for a moment at Bolan, then smiled. "You'll see."

10

The ride into the mountains lasted four more hours, then they passed three well-manned roadblock checkpoints and came to the rebel base camp. It was a permanent installation with frame buildings, an old rancho of some sort and more coffee trees. Bolan and the Russian had said little the rest of the trip. The Executioner had taken a nap and was fresh and ready when the truck stopped.

The Russian laughed, watching Bolan.

"I have never seen a combat soldier relax so completely after an action, nor one come awake so instantly," Aleksandr said. "I would assume you have been in this line of work for some time."

"That's true, friend," Bolan replied. "Whoever pays the best buys my services. You in the market?"

Aleksandr hesitated, then shook his head. "No, I'm afraid not, but the idea is interesting."

The camp commander came up with an entourage of a half-dozen officers, all in crisply pressed fatigues with blocked soft hats like those that Castro made known worldwide.

The head man seemed to be the one with the general's stars on his collar. He threw out his arms and hugged Galkin, then kissed both his cheeks. Galkin returned the traditional greeting.

"My friend! It is good to have you here. The people's party of El Salvador welcomes you. You are our comrade in arms, our loyal and total ally."

The Russian caught some of it, but he looked quickly at Bolan. The Executioner translated the message and Galkin launched into a wordy speech.

Bolan coughed and Galkin looked at him and stopped. Bolan summarized in Spanish what Galkin had said.

As he finished the translation, another man came around the group. He was not as dark as the others, wore a thin mustache and a goatee. He spoke rapidly in Russian, and Galkin moved toward him and hugs ensued.

Bolan caught the introduction. The man's name was Ahmed Hassan. He said he was from Damascus, Syria. The two spoke a moment more, then Aleksandr turned back to the general. Now he let Ahmed translate for him and Bolan edged away. They must talk at once, Aleksandr said to the general. The three went off to the largest building.

Bolan chatted with the men he had come with as they stood around the trucks waiting for orders. The Executioner walked around and peered into both trucks. In one of them he found a curious long box. It was made of heavy wood and had air-shipment tags still on it. A tag in English read Vancouver. He looked closer. The box was eight feet long, nearly three feet square, and open at one end. It was not solid, but rather a frame used for protection during shipments.

He saw a bright shiny steel surface inside the open end. It was a metal cylinder—a canister. The printed matter on the metal was shielded. Bolan jumped up on the tailgate of the truck and sat down, swinging his legs, then reached back and brushed aside some of the soft packing. The letters and numbers glared at him.

PD69CC-HA-DXY-198.

He looked away, slumped against the front of the box, and dropped his head to his chest, pretending to sleep.

It was one of the canisters stolen from the Binder Depository in Idaho...in El Salvador, way up here in the hills.

"Hello there, American," someone said to him in English.

Bolan stretched and opened his eyes.

The man was dressed like the others, but was snapping pictures with a 35mm camera. Two telephoto lenses of different focal lengths hung around his neck on black cords.

"I understand you're the hero of the run. Took on the government forces singlehandedly."

Bolan jumped down from the tailgate. "Just earning my pay. You're not an American."

"I'll have to work on my accent more." He held out his hand. "Davidov, Kusan Davidov. I'm a correspondent for Tass. I want to do a story on you."

"Story is fine, but no pictures. Mercenaries don't like that kind of publicity."

"I understand," Davidov said. "No pictures. I've been talking with the others. How did you get out of that jeep so fast?"

"Lucky," Bolan said. He went over the events, telling it the way it happened. The journalist looked disappointed. "Sorry, Davidov, nothing dramatic or wild. Just another day at the war."

Davidov laughed. "Maybe you'd like to tag along with me on my next little run. Something interesting is happening. That's really why I am here."

"You making the news now?" The Executioner asked.

"I don't make it. But if someone else is going to do something unusual, different, drastic, then I want to be along and record the whole thing for my millions of readers."

"Is it true you Tass guys never get by-lines?"

"Not true at all. But we must have an outstanding story, and the party does not believe in the cult of the individual. So I'll never be a star and be asked to work for the *New York Times*. But I can live with that."

Bolan nodded at the crate. "Would your big story have anything to do with this little gadget in the truck?"

"Well now, you sound like a reporter yourself. I think the chow line is forming. Let's eat. We may be leaving shortly."

Bolan ate. He was hungry, but he was preoccupied with the canister. Would they pick it up with a helicopter and take it back to the capital? That was the only situation he could think of that would rate a special Tass correspondent. And the newsman had been here when the rest of them arrived. So had the Syrian who was on such good terms with the KGB agent. Something big was coming.

Bolan tried to come up with some ideas how to detox the nerve gas, but he could think of no sure way. If it was released into the atmosphere it would vaporize and dissipate—but he had no idea how long it would remain potent.

The food was army style in mess kits. There were even cans of hot soapy water at the far end of the area where everyone washed his own mess gear. They ate a thick bean soup, heavy dark bread, bananas and lots of coffee.

Bolan sat under a tree and watched the troops. They were much like the men in any army. Doing as they were told, waiting for orders, eating and resting while they could, their hands never far from loaded weapons even in a secure situation. These men had lived with death and danger for a long time.

The door on the biggest building opened and the camp commander came out. His nickname was *El Cuchillo*, the Knife. The general, Aleksandr and the Syrian talked for a moment at the front of the building, then the general gave a curt hand signal and a squad of six men stood and jogged to the truck that carried the canister.

The journalist Davidov, who had risen as soon as they came out, now walked to the general and talked with the three for a moment. Bolan saw all of them look in his direction and the KGB man made a mild protest and was overruled. Davidov came jogging back to where Bolan lay.

"We're ready, Scott. You're going to see some news made. I said I wanted you along as my personal bodyguard. I won. You want to go?"

Bolan stood and grinned, slung his M-16 over his shoulder and made sure he had the other three magazines inside his shirt.

"Be crazy not to go on a jaunt like this. We going the whole way by truck or do we get an airlift?"

Davidov chuckled, his double chin bouncing. "I see you have been thinking what the target might be. That's good. I could make you into a fine journalist. But remember the party line. Come, let's get in that first truck."

He and Davidov walked to the first truck and jumped in the back. They found the six troopers opening the crating on the end of the canister. The men removed the one-by-four boards carefully, one at a time, but they seemed to have no fear of the canister.

Bolan suppressed a shiver and looked at Davidov. "You can tell me what's going down now. What the hell is this thing, an atomic bomb?"

Davidov laughed. "Not at all, but it could kill almost as many people if it were in the right spot. We have no such grandiose plans. Just a small experiment, and one that will put shame and humiliation on the U.S. government and cause a worldwide protest against the inhumane monsters who run your country. Just wait and watch."

The only thing that made sense in Bolan's mind was that the rebels were going to use the deadly gas on an innocent village. They would kill innocent women and children, and the Russian would take pictures and record it and send it all to *Pravda* and release it worldwide. At least he could stop it. But even as he thought, a thin wire dropped over his head, tightening around his neck, and another one looped around his chest, pinning his arms to his sides.

He was helpless.

Kusan Davidov smiled at Bolan.

"Scott, my friend. I couldn't take the chance. You might have some deep American loyalties after all, and we can't risk that. You will be restrained until the action is over. Then as soon as I'm out of the camp you will be released."

"I'm a professional mercenary. I don't fight against my employers."

"Mercs have been known to quit the job and change sides. We don't want that to happen. I had to promise this to both the general and our Russian friend, Aleksandr."

After half an hour of more driving, through a roadblock checkpoint and then high along a ridge, they arrived at their destination.

Bolan was taken from the truck and tied to a tree. He could only watch as the soldiers gently let the big crate out of the truck, using a block and tackle. Then they took the rest of the crating away until the canister lay naked on the ridge line.

As he looked at what he could see in the narrow

ravine below, Bolan spotted smoke coming from a camp or a village. He had no idea why there would be so remote a village this deep in the mountains. The men moved the big canister with pry poles until it was at the very lip of the steep canyon, then blocked it with one key log. When the log was pulled, the canister would roll downward.

Davidov seemed to be in charge. He checked the light, then the wind and nodded. One guerrilla taped a hand grenade to the nozzle on the death tank. He put his fingers in the safety ring and looked at Davidov. The Russian journalist nodded, then the rebel pulled the safety pin from the grenade but held the activating handle down. Another man jiggled loose the key log holding the canister in place and it began to roll gently forward. The first man let go of the grenade, the arming handle flipped away and the big canister rolled over the side and down the sharp dropoff. The men rushed away from the lip. Four seconds after the handle spun away, the grenade blew.

Bolan knew it would be more than powerful enough to blast away the valve and the nozzle, allowing the deadly nerve gas to gush out of the tank. Kurtzman had said it killed in five seconds.

There was a cheer from one man brave enough to look over the edge.

"It blew it off, the gas comes out!" he shouted.

Davidov edged up to the ridge line. The wind was still strong away from them. He smiled and hooked up his 500mm telephoto lens and began taking pictures. They were all in living color and would be sent via TV satellite to Moscow.

Bolan struggled against the ropes. He loosened one but the man watching him tightened it again. The Executioner felt helpless. There was nothing he could do. But he would do everything to stop Davidov from getting his story and his pictures out.

Five minutes later Davidov came back to Bolan.

"What a story! Do you know what is down there? It is an advance camp of about fifty guerrillas. They were all men loyal to Colonel Alvarez. You probably don't know that the colonel has been plotting a coup. He wanted to take over the rebel army for himself and execute the general. We eliminated two problems at once!"

"The gas has killed them?"

"Marvelous! I just saw it. Five seconds after the cloud hit the camp, every man will have been dead. The cloud hung like a dirty blanket over the camp. Now it has moved slowly down the canyon, but there are no civilians for fifteen miles. By then it will be so dissipated that the most it can do is make someone mildly ill."

"How many men did you just kill?"

"About fifty. And you should see the pictures I got. We were well upwind of the gas at all times. We reached within one hundred feet of the camp."

"You should get a Hero First Class medal, you butcher."

"You see, I was afraid you might have second thoughts. A conscience."

"I just like a fair fight. One on one. Or in your

case, your six backup soldiers and you against me. Any time.''

"Sorry, we won't be able to do that. We drive back to that last checkpoint, then I take the truck and head for town. I should have no problem getting through. They don't worry about rigs going the other way. I may have to hike around some of the government checkpoints, but I'll make it. I'll take three of the nonuniformed men with me. You, poor man, are going to have to walk back to the base camp. But you'll have three men to help guard you, so it should go all right. Oh, give my thanks to the general and to Aleksandr Galkin. Strange, I knew him in Moscow. We were both in a KGB school for a while, then I was transferred into journalism.''

Bolan felt them untying him.

He would not resist. Not yet, not until he was back at the base camp.

He had done nothing yet to make them distrust him.

But his time would come.

11

The point where the rebel truck turned south was only four miles from the base camp. Bolan and the three men walked it quickly. The rebel soldiers saw no reason to distrust the Mack Scott who had fought for them at the ambush, and quickly returned his M-16 and the magazines. They even joked about his being tied up during the attack.

With the start that Davidov had, there was no way of catching him, unless Bolan could steal one of the trucks. The damage was done. Even if Davidov could be stopped, someone else would tell about the slaughter and that it was the result of American nerve gas. The only thing to do now was stick with Aleksandr Galkin and find the remaining five canisters.

When they came into camp, the senior noncom reported to the general and to Galkin and the Syrian who had become his shadow. Both were elated. Bolan had watched the exchange in the shaded area near one of the buildings.

"Now, General, it is time that Ahmed and I move on. We have much more work to do together."

"You have given our cause a great and powerful tool," the general said, and Ahmed translated.

"We will make all the political gain from it that we can. We send our thanks to our Marxist brethren in Europe, Russia and of course in the Middle East."

Bolan was trying to get closer to the trio when a distinctive American voice bellowed from an adjoining building.

"Goddammit, man, you have to hold still. How the hell do you expect me to get the needle in your arm?"

The Executioner sauntered toward the building. There were no guards, and once inside he saw why. It was the camp sick bay. Half a dozen men lay on cots under blankets. Three stood waiting to see the man at the table where he worked in a patch of sunlight from an open window.

The large American made an injection, joked about the cry of pain and told the man in perfect Spanish that he would live to father a hundred more children.

One man with a rifle near the far door was the only hint of a guard in the area. As Bolan approached the medic he had no idea who he was; American for sure. A medical doctor, a medical missionary?

He moved toward the doctor, watching the guard who seemed unconcerned. The Executioner stopped a pair of long steps away. He had seen the face before, but he couldn't place it.

"Doctor, where are you from?"

The man's head snapped up, his eyes curious. Surprise tinged his face.

"I might ask the same," he said, after giving

Bolan a cursory glance and then looking back at the patient with a bullet wound in his thigh. "Damn, look at that infection, and all I have is some old sulfa. We need antibiotics and penicillin. How can I get these wounds healed?"

"I came from Miami," Bolan said, restraining the soldier as the doctor continued to probe. The man screamed, and Bolan held him fast.

"Thanks for the help. Nobody else would do that job, and naturally we have no anesthetics. Damn, I wish I had some equipment! There's a man over there who is dying and I can't do anything about it."

"Where did you come from, doctor? You weren't here a few hours ago."

"I had a special ride on a horse around the government forces and almost broke my backside. I haven't been on a horse in twenty years."

"Then you came in from San Salvador. Do you have a name?"

"Yes, A.E. Johnson. Medical doctor by trade."

"You're not here by choice, are you, Dr. Johnson?"

"No, but what difference does that make?"

Some of Bolan's background reading had paid off. Newspaper and magazine accounts had extensively quoted officials on the scene in Central America. The name clicked. Bolan watched the doctor paint the wound with a salve with some minor antibiotics in it, and then make a dressing from the bedsheet.

"Mr. Ambassador, did they kidnap you?"

Dr. Johnson looked up quickly. "Don't call me that, even in English. I just may be able to stay alive if these guerrillas decide I am of more value to them as a doctor than as a corpse."

"When did they capture you?" Bolan said, his voice low, as they walked away from the groaning patient.

"Yesterday morning. It was supposed to be a meeting. They have not mistreated me, but I see no real chance that I can stay alive."

"I can help you." Quickly he told the official about the canister of nerve gas and all the implications. Then he saw the guard walking toward them.

"I need to make some plans," he whispered, "check out some things. As soon as it gets dark, we will make a move."

Bolan met the guard and gave him a cigarette from a pack he carried for just such a situation. He chatted with the sentry about how well the American doctor was doing, then left. He saw the Syrian at the mess area and joined him. They talked first in Russian, then English.

"I think my English is better than your Russian," said the Syrian, smiling.

"Good. My Russian is limited," Bolan said. "I was wondering if you'll be needing any help in your next mission. This one looks about done for me. I've never worked the Middle East. Is there any chance of employment there?"

Ahmed Hassan stared at Bolan for a moment.

"I have heard that you are extremely good at your work. It is true that from time to time we might have need for a resourceful American with your talents, but only if we could be certain of his loyalty." Ahmed paused.

"Hey, I sign a contract, I deliver. No way I change sides in the middle of a deal. Bad for my reputation that way, and I make it or go under by my reputation. You can trust me."

"You do seem to be a man of your word." He hesitated again. The Executioner waited.

"An extremely loyal infidel can always be useful in my business. If you are ever in Damascus, with or without a passport, and need work, look me up. Here is an address that I often use. These people will not admit it, but they can always find me or get a message to me. It may take a week or more. In Damascus we are not in the rush you Americans always seem to be. Look me up if ever you are there."

Bolan wanted to ask him about the five other canisters. Where would they be used? But he knew that would be a mistake. He touched his hand to his forehead in a mock salute. Hassan had written in Arabic both the address and the building name. Bolan tucked the paper into the buttoned top pocket of his jacket and walked toward the chow line. It was time for food again.

The Executioner ate because the others did. For the next few hours he did not want to attract any attention. While he ate he saw the Syrian and the Russian KGB agent leave in an ancient Ford station wagon.

He first heard the rumor in the chow line. The ambassador was to be executed that night. Then it was delayed until tomorrow when a man with a camera would record the final moments of the warmongering United States Ambassador. Tomorrow for sure!

The combatman ambled around the camp until he had every aspect of the place memorized. The motor pool was down to one vehicle, one of the trucks that had brought them. He found a small tent where grenades and a few land mines were stored.

The Central American night had fallen quickly, and now it was black. Visiting the improvised hospital, Bolan found the doctor working on the less seriously ill by the light of a gas lantern. The ailments were sprains, sore throats and rashes. Bolan whispered to the doctor.

"We leave in thirty minutes. The signal will be an explosion, which should be spectacular. When you hear it, head to the top of the trail, where it comes into the camp, and keep in the shadows."

"You have a plan that will work?"

"It had better. Your execution is set for noon tomorrow."

The doctor nodded, checked another patient. "I should have known. Politics was always stronger than medicine. I don't even know your name."

"Mack Scott."

"All right, Scott. I'll close up here and try to work my way near to the gate. Good luck. Your country will thank you for this, if we get out of here alive."

"We have to, Mr. Ambassador. I have an appointment in Damascus."

IN THE DARKNESS, BOLAN FOUND no guards around the truck. He checked his time. Quickly he hot-wired the engine so a touch of the wires under the hood would kick over the starter. Quietly he lowered the hood and moved around to the pup tent where the hand grenades were kept. Right there he would have given fifty thousand dollars for a ten-minute timer. Instead he had a four-second timer. The truck was located a little uphill from the pup tent, some sixty yards. It was pointed downhill toward the gate, fifty yards below the pup tent.

He found what he needed in the truck, a small ball of twine. With the cord he could have a running start. Five minutes before his departure, Bolan eased into the area just behind the tent, pulled up the back flap and reached inside for the hand grenades. They were in a box. He took one out, tied the string loosely around the grenade, including the arming handle, and pulled the safety pin.

Cautiously Bolan let up on the arming handle. It touched the cord and held. The slightest tug on the line would pull the cord off the handle, the handle would pop off and arm the bomb. Four seconds later, it would explode. The Executioner put the booby-trapped grenade back in the box of other grenades and played the string out carefully. He left slack and laid it out in a straight line toward the truck. The cord was sixty feet long. So short!

He left the end under a rock and walked through the darkness. A roving guard called to him. He called back in Spanish, saying he was the American who could not sleep.

The guard grunted and Bolan went on to the truck. He eased into the cab and without closing the door, let off the emergency brake and pushed the gearshift into neutral. The two-ton truck squeaked and groaned and rolled forward slowly. He touched the brake once to keep the speed and the noise down. Gradually the big black hulk rolled to where he knew the rock had to be. He let it go a little farther.

The Executioner eased on the brake, then pulled the emergency brake and jumped to the ground. The guard was beside him.

"What the hell you doing?" the guard asked.

Bolan had put the M-16 over his shoulder, muzzle up, when he left the cab and now he pivoted, pulling the sling and slamming the butt plate of the weapon into the guard's chin. The man groaned. Bolan kicked him in the crotch, then drove his foot into the guard's chest as he fell to the ground. The nightfighter's heavy boot smashed through ribs, driving a broken bone into the guard's heart, killing him instantly.

At the back of the truck, the Executioner found the rock and the string, which he gently tugged a foot farther and tied to the tailgate. At the front of the truck he lifted the hood and touched the wires. The engine ground once, twice, then caught. He dropped the hood, leaped into the truck and gunned the accelerator, slammed into gear and released the brake. The truck tumbled forward toward the gate.

Bolan could almost see the string slip off the arming spoon, and then four seconds later....

Behind him the grenade exploded, detonating thirty-two cases of grenades and land mines. It was a horrendous, gut-punching blast, with shrapnel from five hundred grenades flying everywhere, slicing into flesh, digging into buildings and trees. The sky lit up with the exploding grenades as they turned the silent night into death thunder. Behind him, trigger-happy guards began to shoot at nothing and everything.

The truck careered toward the gate. He pulled on the lights and saw the ambassador appear from behind some brush and step a dozen paces to the road. Bolan flashed the lights as a signal and slammed on the brakes, throwing the truck into a skid as the doctor jumped on the running board and climbed inside. At once Bolan jammed the accelerator to the floorboards.

Dr. Johnson pushed the M-16 out his side of the truck. Points of light showed ahead as the rebels began firing. Dr. Johnson sent a 5-round burst at the lights, then another, and all but one stopped firing.

Then the truck was at the small barricade, a single six-inch log mounted on a counterweight to be swung aside. The lock was a half-inch bolt through a metal holder. The truck crashed through, scattering the remaining guards as it roared down the trail.

Neither occupant of the truck had said a word. Shots sounded from behind but they had a fifteen-foot wooden box at the back to absorb the bullets.

"Made it, by damn!" Ambassador Johnson shouted.

"First hurdle. There are three more checkpoints down the road, all rebel. I don't think they have radio, so we should be a big surprise. We'll play the game the same way." Bolan handed the doctor the other magazines.

He drove the bumpy trail as fast as he could, but still twenty to twenty-five miles an hour was the best he could do. Dr. Johnson, watching the rear, said he saw no lights following them.

The first checkpoint was unmanned and the barrier was raised. By the time they were through it, one man staggered from the shack at the side of the road and shouted.

More than an hour later, Bolan recognized the next roadblock. Twin sets of logs were dug deep into the road, and vehicles had to slow and turn to one side or the other. It was a sharp angle and cut the speed to five mph.

As they approached, a flare shot into the air. It burst over them. Bolan waved a hand out the side of the truck.

"We'll have to bluff this one," he said. "If they get too curious, use that thing."

Dr. Johnson nodded grimly. He had already put in a full magazine.

Bolan brought the rig almost to a stop, geared down and made the first turn to the right around the poles. A rebel soldier jumped on the driver's running board and looked inside as they continued moving.

"I have some seriously injured in the back," Bolan barked in Spanish. "Got to get them to a doctor in San Salvador or they die. You should have been told."

"Nobody told me!" the guard said. "You got papers?"

"Hell no, no time!" Bolan said.

"Stop and I'll check," the guard said, waving his pistol.

They had made it past the second row of posts.

"Yeah, I'll stop," Bolan said. "You got any coffee inside?"

The guard, still on the running board of the truck, waved at three men near the quick turn back to the main road, smooth and wide here, and the men lowered their guns. Bolan tensed his foot over the accelerator.

"Now!" he shouted. The ambassador brought up the M-16 and chattered three rounds into the guard's chest. The sound inside the cab was deafening as the rounds flew inches from Bolan's face and out the window to hit the guard. He fell from the truck. One of the guards ahead prepared to fire, but Bolan swung the truck back on the road, smashing him with the fender. Bolan felt a bump as the big tires rolled over the guy.

Then they were back on the road, roaring forward, with nothing ahead but one small checkpoint and the risk of bypassing government forces without passwords or credentials.

"Let's hope we don't run into an ambush where the troops fire first and ask questions second," the Executioner said.

"It couldn't happen, Scott. We've been too lucky so far to get cut up by friendly forces."

They made it through the last checkpoint without

trouble: evidently both guards were sleeping. Bolan blinked the lights on and off every two minutes as they drove. It would be unusual for a vehicle to do so if it were trying to go unnoticed. It was the only thing the Executioner could think of to help them make soft contact with the troops below. What he did not want was a shoulder-mounted rocket launcher to put a missile into the truck.

They had just passed the spot where the ambush had occurred on the trip up, when Bolan slowed the truck and began blinking the lights and blowing the horn. At last he figured it. He hit the horn in the international Morse code: three shorts, three longs, three shorts. He waited several seconds and repeated the signal.

Dr. Johnson looked at him and smiled. "That's an SOS. Do you think any of these people were Boy Scouts?"

"I hope to hell they were."

They drove another two miles at fifteen mph. The Executioner figured he had sent the SOS out more than a hundred times when he saw lights flashing ahead. He flashed the lights in the SOS code again. He waited and the same short, long, short signals came back.

Slowly he edged the truck ahead. He stopped blowing the horn. At a hundred yards the lights were glaring. Bolan hit the dimmer switch and slanted the lights downward. Someone in the other rig did the same. He drove to within twenty-five feet of the other vehicle and stopped. Slowly he stepped out of the rig, hands over his head.

"We are friends," the nightfighter shouted in Spanish. "Please send out your officer. I have an important passenger."

There was a long pause, and Bolan repeated his words in Spanish. A figure moved forward cautiously. Bolan moved forward too, hands in the air. Slowly the figure took shape, and the Executioner saw the uniform.

Government forces!

12

It was nearly dawn before the El Salvador government forces' truck arrived at the United States Embassy and let out the ambassador and Bolan. They had telephoned at the first phone. Lights were on all over the compound. Guards were at every gate. Heavy trucks were parked in front of the driveways. Every U.S. Marine on duty at the embassy was wearing combat gear.

The ambassador's wife ran to her husband, tears flowing and eyes glistening with joy.

Bolan was taken to a private room, told he could sleep, shower, eat, take a bath, have a drink, do whatever he wanted. The ambassador would talk with him at ten o'clock.

The Executioner thanked the uniformed attendant, ordered a steak sandwich and a cold beer, then took a half-hour shower. He came out relaxed and sleepy. He put on shorts and dived into the bed, ready for sleep. The clock on the dresser showed him that it was 6:00 A.M. He programmed himself to wake up at nine-thirty and went to sleep at once.

JUST AFTER TEN THAT MORNING, Bolan sat in the ambassador's private office. The medic looked refreshed. He couldn't help smiling at his rescuer.

"I don't need to know if you're with some government agency or not, Scott. I figure if you wanted me to know, you'd have told me. My guess is you're not official or I would have known it by now."

The ambassador got up and walked to the window. He stared through the iron bars at the concrete block wall of the outer courtyard. "I don't know what the hell I'm doing here in El Salvador. The President insisted that I take this spot, and I guess I've helped smooth some rough edges. But I'm no damned diplomat. I should be in the hospital downtown lecturing and helping the young medical students."

He shrugged and returned to his chair. "This morning I put through a signal to Washington, commending you for your work, asking for a medal of honor for you. They usually don't issue them in peacetime, but this wasn't exactly peaceful. I put down your name as Mack Scott as you said. If that's not your real name, it doesn't matter. I've had your gear brought around from your hotel."

"Thank you, Mr. Ambassador."

There was no one else in the room.

"Now onto your plans, then. I would like to put in a bid for your services," Dr. Johnson said. "I need a better bodyguard than I've had down here, as you found out. I want to put you on staff as a GS-13 at thirty-six thousand a year, beginning the first of last month."

"Mr. Ambassador...."

"Please let me finish. You will have a car and driver at your command, as well as an apartment here in the embassy. Your only job will be watching my tail and keeping me out of trouble. You damn well saved my neck back there. I'm not good at this sort of thing. A man does not take it lightly when someone saves his life. I'm not a man of violence. I'm not used to it, I don't like it. I know I killed one man, perhaps more than one last night. But it was them or us, him or me. A man thinks differently in those situations. I want you to see to it that I don't get in any more trouble like that."

He paused to look at his watch, then continued. "Don't say a word right now. Go back to your room and relax, then have lunch and a nap and we'll meet for dinner in my quarters at seven. This is tremendously important to me."

Bolan got up and shook the ambassador's hand and went to his room down the long hallway.

In the room he checked his battered suitcase. It was intact. The traveler's checks were still in the suitcase lining, the cash still sewn in his sport coat.

He found a pen and paper, and wrote a note to the ambassador apologizing for having to leave. He indicated he was still on the track of the rest of the gas and it was important for him to follow Aleksandr Galkin the KGB agent and Hassan the Syrian as quickly as he could.

An hour later Bolan caught a flight to Miami.

As the plane took off, he relaxed. Now that he was away, he intended to use a different name, so the ambassador would have to do the best he could to find him.

The Executioner turned on the soft music in his earphones and let his mind drift back.

He had been nervous on that tiny piece of American soil in El Salvador. The embassy had shielded him, but it had also been a hazard, the ever present chance that someone there might know him, might connect him with Colonel John Phoenix and the wanted notices out on him by the CIA.

Now the Executioner could relax fully. He was on his own again. He lived for the day when he could bring the KGB mastermind Major General Greb Strakhov into his control. The Russian general had been the man who had worked out the plan that ended Colonel John Phoenix's useful operations for the United States government. It was Strakhov who was responsible for the death of April Rose. It was Strakhov who had devised and executed the plan to kill the labor leader in the Warsaw pact nation and blame it on Phoenix.

Bolan had been grievously wounded in the spirit by April Rose's death at Stony Man Farm. He dropped the John Phoenix pose and worked his way to Moscow, where he stayed for months with the Russian "underground" of Gypsies, dissidents and small-time criminals. They sheltered him, helped provide for him as he tried to uncover who had carried out the plot against Stony Man Farm and against John Phoenix. Once he knew that, he could vindicate himself.

When he learned at last the name of Major General Greb Strakhov, the highly placed KGB leader was out of reach. It was then that he found out that a helicopter pilot John Phoenix had killed in Afghanistan had been the general's son. Only then did Bolan know why the general hated Colonel John Phoenix so fiercely.

But even with the facts about the plot against him revealed, Bolan did not succeed in clearing his name. He tracked down the mole, the American spying for the Soviets in a rival American intelligence agency, who had set up Stony Man Farm for the attack where April Rose had been killed. Bolan had captured the mole, shown his complicity and executed him in the Oval Office with the President as a witness.

The killing destroyed Bolan's last chance to return to any kind of good graces with the American establishment. Now Stony Man Farm and all its resources were totally beyond his reach. Now the KGB, the Western intelligence agencies, and even the CIA were hunting him.

As in the old days, Mack Bolan was the outsider looking in, waging a solo war for justice against tremendous odds. He had to do it all, facing an utterly hostile world alone. But he had to do it, he had no choice. In his mercy, he would kill—and kill *personally*—to help restore the balance of right and wrong. His wounds were personal, and it was he personally who suffered so gravely when the balance of righteousness was upset and the snakes of evil and terror unloosed on the world. So he would fight a personal war.

As the pilot announced that they were starting their descent into Miami, the Executioner was disturbed. It was as if he had been reading a mystery novel and twenty pages of the book were missing.

How did he know that the other canisters were going to Syria?

He did not know. He assumed it. He had made one of those combat decisions that must be right or you are dead.

Was he wrong? Why should the gas go to Syria?

He thought about his intuitive conclusion. Why else would a Syrian be at the "test site" in El Salvador? The Syrians were the logical customer for the other five canisters. They were on a wartime footing. They had combat troops in action every day. They had men on the lines. They were fighting their historic and hated enemy, Israel, and simultaneously trying to stabilize Lebanon and keep the many factions in that war-shattered nation in line. Bolan knew from Kurtzman that his good friends in Able Team were even now involved in a fantastic war in the Middle East, where Syrians, Iranians, Libyans and American black nationalists were embroiled in a smorgasbord of blood and violence, their only political unity being the groups' lust for terror.

In such an environment, Bolan decided that the ultimate target for the gas would not be Lebanon or the Druse or the other factions fighting there. The only logical target for the gas was Israel. With five canisters, the Syrians could attack the five largest Israeli cities. The chemicals could be released by special aircraft over the cities at night to produce genocide by morning. By the time his plane landed, Bolan had devised a plan and fixed it clearly in his mind.

Bolan gathered together his gear and waited until everyone was lined up in the aisle. Then he walked off. As usual, everyone had to wait at the luggage carousel for the bags to arrive. Bolan spent his time calling the various consulates in Miami until he found the one that handled Syria.

No problem, he could leave on an evening plane.

13

Mack Bolan had never enjoyed international travel. Airports, jet liners, more airports, customs inspectors and hassles over baggage were not his idea of having fun. After two delays, he arrived in Damascus a day and a half after leaving Miami, which was about average, as another American in the customs line told him.

The Executioner had been surprised by the green around Damascus. Somehow he thought of Syria and most of the Middle East as one huge desert. The Barada river runs through the heart of Damascus and is the source of water for the city as well as for extensive surrounding irrigation in fields of fruits. The city had seemed to float into view as an extension of the barren eastern slopes of some mountains.

Bolan declared his cash and traveler's checks, did not mention the cash sewn into his jacket and was cleared quickly. He had no weapons, not even a pen knife, and he had a feeling he would have to do something about that quickly.

The friendly American in the customs line told the big man with the ice-hard eyes he was going to the best hotel in town and even that was not anything special. The Executioner's Arabic was almost nonexistent and he asked the American if he could ride along. It was the Hotel Gamil, which his English-speaking friend said meant beautiful. It was. They introduced themselves. The small, balding American's name was Harry Engeland, from Boston on a vacation. On this occasion Bolan used his passport name, Mack Scott.

He registered, found an English-speaking employee and told him what he wanted. The man nodded and wrote down an address. Bolan showed it to a taxi driver and was let out in front of a small shop in the bazaar section of town.

Quickly he found the first item he wanted: a walking cane, sturdy but not overpowering. It cost eight Syrian pounds, a little over two dollars, had fancy carving on it and was highly varnished. In another store he purchased a small pocketknife. It took the Executioner half an hour to find the rest of what he needed. At last he located a shop with fishing equipment and bought a fifty-yard roll of thirty-pound clear monofilament fishing line. It had a slight blue tinge but would work well, the Executioner decided.

Back in the hotel he completed his passive weapon. He notched a ring around the tip of the cane with the small knife, then tightly knotted the end of the nylon line around it. He measured off an arm's length of the nylon, then one more, cut off the line and tied a two-inch loop in the end and bent the line back on itself, pushing it through the loop, forming a noose. Now he adjusted the length of the noose so he could form a circle two feet in diameter and be able to keep it three feet from the end of the cane.

When it was perfectly formed, Bolan retied the end of the line on the tip of the cane and stretched the loop and the single strand along the length of the cane. He bound the fishing line in place with spots of cellophane tape and was pleased with his unconventional yet highly effective weapon, a garrote on a stick. The plastic line was hard to see from a few feet away.

Next he took from his pocket the address that Ahmed Hassan had given him and went out to find a taxi. The driver looked at the address and asked Bolan something.

"La yatakalam," the Executioner said. His American friend Engeland told him that meant, "I don't speak." It worked. The driver shrugged and charged into the crazy Damascus traffic. A million and a half people live in the capital of Syria, and all of them seemed to want to take this street at the same time with cars, trucks, bicycles and a few donkeys and camels.

Bolan had never seen anything like it. Minor scrapes and bumps of fenders and body panels were ignored as the drivers jockeyed, charged and bluffed for position.

At last they came to a narrower and less traveled street. The taxi driver stopped a dozen numbers down from the address Bolan had given him and said something. The Executioner didn't understand. The driver snatched the bills offered. So much for over-tipping.

Bolan recognized the large and plain Arabic lettering from Hassan's note and saw that the building was an office of some sort. Without hesitation, he pushed the door open and walked in.

The quiet inside surprised him. No hawking from the street vendors, no snarl of traffic, no blaring of horns. He found himself on a deep-pile carpet in a beautifully decorated room about ten feet square. An attractive woman behind a desk looked up from some papers and asked him something in Arabic.

"Do you speak English?" he asked.

"Yes, of course. How may I assist you?"

She was striking. She had deep-set dark eyes, heavy lashes and her black hair coiled and fastened to one side.

"I'm looking for Ahmed Hassan. I met him a few days ago in El Salvador. He said if I made it to Damascus I should contact him. He indicated that he might have some work for me."

"Mr. Hassan is not here. We have had no word from him for some time, but if you wish to leave your name and the name of the hotel where you are staying, we will let him know at our first chance."

"Good. I'm Mack Scott, staying at the Gamil hotel."

She wrote something on a red three-by-five card.

"Thank you, Mr. Scott. I'll see that Mr. Hassan gets your message if we can contact him."

Bolan returned to the street. The taxi he had used before sat in front of the building. Bolan got in and told the driver to return to the hotel. All he needed was the one word, and the driver understood.

The big American waited in his room. There was no call. At four that afternoon he left the hotel and

HE'S EXPLOSIVE. HE'S MACK BOLAN... AGAINST ALL ODDS

He learned his deadly skills in Vietnam...then put them to good use by destroying the Mafia in a blazing one-man war. Now **Mack Bolan** ventures further into the cold to take on his deadliest challenge yet—the KGB's worldwide terror machine.

Follow the lone warrior on his exciting new missions...and get ready for more nonstop action from his high-powered combat teams: **Able Team**—Bolan's famous Death Squad—battling urban savagery too brutal and volatile for regular law enforcement. And **Phoenix Force**—five extraordinary warriors handpicked by Bolan to fight the dirtiest of antiterrorist wars, blazing into even greater danger.

Fight alongside these three courageous forces for freedom in all-new action-packed novels! Travel to the gloomy depths of the cold Atlantic, the scorching sands of the Sahara, and the desolate Russian plains. You'll feel the pressure and excitement building page after page, with nonstop action that keeps you enthralled until the explosive conclusion!

Now you can have all the new Gold Eagle novels delivered right to your home!

You won't want to miss a single one of these exciting new action-adventures. And you don't have to! Just fill out and mail the card at right, and we'll enter your name in the Gold Eagle home subscription plan. You'll then receive six brand-new action-packed Gold Eagle books every other month, delivered right to your home! You'll get two Mack Bolan novels, one Able Team and one Phoenix Force, plus one book each from two thrilling, new Gold Eagle libraries, **SOBs** and **Track**. In **SOBs** you'll meet the legendary team of mercenary warriors who fight for justice and win. **Track** features a military and weapons genius on a mission to stop a maniac whose dream is everybody's worst nightmare. Only Track stands between us and nuclear hell!

FREE! The New War Book and Mack Bolan bumper sticker.

As soon as we receive your card we'll rush you the long-awaited New War Book and Mack Bolan bumper sticker—both ABSOLUTELY FREE with your first six Gold Eagle novels.

The New War Book is *packed* with exciting information for Bolan fans: a revealing look at the hero's life...two new short stories...book character biographies...even a combat catalog describing weapons used in the novels! The New War Book is a special collector's item you'll want to read again and again. And it's yours FREE when you mail your card!

Of course, you're under no obligation to buy anything. Your first six books come on a 10-day free trial—if you're not thrilled with them, just return them and owe nothing. The New War Book and bumper sticker are yours to keep, FREE!

Don't miss a single one of these thrilling novels...mail the card now, while you're thinking about it.

HE'S UNSTOPPABLE.
AND HE'LL FIGHT
TO DEFEND FREEDOM!

FREE! THE NEW WAR BOOK AND
MACK BOLAN BUMPER STICKER
when you join our home subscription plan.

Gold Eagle Reader Service, a Division of Worldwide Library
2504 West Southern Avenue, Tempe, Arizona 85282

YES, rush me my FREE New War Book and Mack Bolan bumper sticker and my
first six Gold Eagle novels. These first seven books are mine to examine free for
10 days. If I am not entirely satisfied with these books, I will return the six books
within 10 days and owe nothing. If I decide to keep these novels, I will pay just
$1.95 per book (total $11.70). I will then receive the six Gold Eagle novels every
other month, and will be billed the same low price of $11.70 per shipment.
I understand that each shipment will contain two Mack Bolan novels, and one
each from the Able Team, Phoenix Force, SOBs and Track libraries. There are no
shipping and handling or any other hidden charges. I may cancel this arrange-
ment at any time, and The New War Book and bumper sticker are mine to keep
as gifts, even if I do not buy any additional books.

166-CIM-PAEH

Name	(please print)	
Address		Apt. No.
City	State	Zip
Signature	(If under 18, parent or guardian must sign.)	

This offer limited to one order per household. We reserve the right to exercise
discretion in granting membership. Offer expires June 30, 1985.

PRINTED IN U.S.A.

GET THE NEW WAR BOOK AND
BUMPER STICKER
FREE!

See exciting
details inside.

again took a taxi to the address Hassan had given him. This time he stayed well back, made sure the driver did not return and watched the front door. Just after five o'clock, the tall, slender woman emerged and walked away.

The Executioner followed her. She walked rapidly, not watching to see if anyone were following her; as far as Bolan could tell, no one else was. She went up several blocks, through a main artery and into a better section of town where she entered an apartment complex. He got close enough to see her press a numbered button and go past a heavy door, which locked behind her.

He leaned against a closed shop and waited for two hours. She did not come out. Bolan was hungry, tired and slightly angry that he was at a dead end. He had to find Hassan soon or it would be too late. He expected the Syrian would strike quickly. They had been waiting for centuries for a chance like this to annihilate the Jews. Now they had the right weapon.

Bolan turned and almost bumped into a small dark-haired woman with big sunglasses. A smart white linen suit covered her well-proportioned figure.

She glanced up at him, smiled and put her arm through his and matched his slow stride.

"I was afraid you would stay here all evening. There is nothing to learn of Hassan this way, but there are other ways. You are the American who arrived this morning, is staying at the Gamil and wishes he could speak Arabic. I speak the language like a native. You are using the name Mack Scott, obvious-

ly an alias. Now that we have that out of the way, are
you ready for some dinner?''

Bolan tried to smile. He had been surprised by the
woman's presence, startled when she took his arm
and stunned that she knew all about him. It came too
suddenly, so he laughed.

''Now, miss. If we could try this all again. My
name is Mack Scott, I'm a plastics salesman from
Peoria, and you're right about my not speaking the
language. What's this about Hassan?''

She lifted one dark brow, took off her sunglasses
and put them in a pocket in the lightweight jacket.

''First we'll have dinner. I know a special spot,
and I can even find a hamburger for you if you insist.
We can talk shop as we go along. I have been following you and watching you since you visited Hassan's
blind drop this morning. It would be a favor of me to
suggest that you find a better spot than the lining of
your jacket for the spare cash you carry.''

Bolan looked at her and this time his laugh was full
and hearty. He hadn't been away from his room for
more than ten minutes since she had tailed him back
there this morning. She must be good or had help.

''I'd love to have some dinner. Do you have a
name? An alias will do.''

''Now that is better. My name is Luana, it is German and Hebrew, and we will talk more later when
the walls do not have ears.''

She signaled and an old Renault drove up. She
reached for the door; Bolan beat her to it and followed her inside. She spoke rapidly in Arabic and the
car surged ahead.

"Yes, I too have been watching for Ahmed Hassan or any of his friends. My last information was that he was in the Western Hemisphere somewhere."

"Who are you?"

"I work with friends of the United States," she said. "We both struggle for the betterment of the world, not its destruction."

"Israeli intelligence?"

"Surely you realize that I can say neither yes or no. But we must work together. I could guess you are CIA or M-6, but I think neither. There is a strange, independent air about you." She smiled and her brown eyes shone. Her hair, loose around her shoulders, shaded one cheek.

The car stopped at the curb and they got out at a dimly lit alley. She took his arm and marched him down a series of stone steps, through a beaded curtain into a dungeonlike room decorated in silks and pillows and small tables, with flickering candles in chandeliers. There were no electric lights. It looked like the inside of a sultan's desert tent, or perhaps that of his favorite wife.

A robed waiter led them to a table, where he seated Bolan and let Luana sit down by herself.

"Remember," she said, when Bolan stared at the waiter, "that in the Arab world, a woman is a third-class citizen, coming after the man, his male sons and his sports car if he has one. Then his wife."

"My three wives would never accept that," Bolan said.

"Good," she said, laughing softly. "This is the

type of business where a little humor helps. Here there are ears in every cushion. We will talk nothing of our problem, only eat, enjoy the dancer if there is one tonight and then leave. We talk later.''

She ordered for them in fluid Arabic, and it was plain that the waiter knew her. There were small crackers and some kind of cheese and a soup he didn't want to know the contents of. When the lamb came, it was cooked to perfection and he enjoyed it. They had three kinds of tea and for dessert a watery pudding.

Bolan had found out little about her at the meal. Every time he asked a question she shook her head silently, although there was no one within hearing distance.

He paid the bill, and outside she found transport quickly. It was not a taxi, he discovered, but the same car and driver who had taken them to the restaurant.

As soon as the door closed she began talking seriously.

"Hassan is back in Damascus. I found that out this morning. He is traveling with a Russian who is using a special diplomatic passport.''

"The Russian's name is Galkin, KGB. I met him in El Salvador,'' Bolan said. "You do know about the canister of poison nerve gas they used down there?''

"Everyone knows about that. The papers and the radio have been overflowing with it. Depending on your politics, the U.S. is the biggest warmonger since Napoleon, or an unwitting and bumbling idiot.''

"And why are you watching Hassan?'' he asked.

"We always watch Hassan. I am acquainted with him, and with some of the other more ambitious of the Syrian power team. They think I am Arab and I do not discourage that. I am only one-quarter Arab, but do not tell them."

"And you have access to the inner workings of the Syrian military, their intelligence operation?"

"Only on the periphery, the crumbs. Anything helps these days."

"Do the Syrians have war games planned? Do they have a contingency plan for driving the Israelis into the sea?"

She laughed as the car hurtled through the streets. "Of course. Every Arab nation in the world has half a dozen. They are wish machines, fantasies."

"Do any of the Syrian fantasies include the use of poison gas?"

She caught his arm. "Do not play games with me. The Russians stole the gas from the United States, at least that is our guess. Then used it in El Salvador to discredit the United States. Now you are here and you know Hassan and the Russian KGB man. Why are you in Syria? Is there a connection with the gas?" She stared at him in the bouncing car. "Was more than one canister of the nerve gas stolen?"

"Six were stolen in a vicious attack on a storage facility. None have been recaptured. One was used."

The car stopped in front of a low building. It was fully dark now. She motioned. "Come, we have much work to do, you and I. I will introduce you to some people, and we will talk and plan. We must prevent the massacre of a whole nation."

14

Ahmed Hassan stood in front of a plain wooden table in a top-secret office at the Atsi military air base just outside Damascus. He smiled at the six men gathered there, the best planners and strategists in the Syrian military establishment. Hassan wore his military uniform, the brigadier stars shining on his shoulders. There were two colonels and another brigadier and two three-star generals sitting around the table. At the far side sat Aleksandr Galkin.

"Good evening, gentlemen. It is set. We have total approval by our president, prime minister and the war council. Now it is up to us. For those of you who have not met our new friend from Moscow, let me present Colonel Aleksandr Galkin, one of the top men in the KGB and second in line to be advanced into the Politburo, the governing authority in the Soviet Union."

Galkin stood, nodded. "I am honored to be here, gentlemen. I will offer any assistance that I can."

He sat down and Hassan thanked him.

"We have word that our special cargo aircraft has cleared Halifax on its second leg from Vancouver, British Columbia, in Canada. It is now scheduled to fly directly to Lisbon, Portugal, for refueling, then nonstop to this field here in Damascus. We expect that the cargo will arrive late tonight, if everything goes well.''

"What might go wrong?'' a colonel asked.

"I'm not even thinking about that, Colonel. We have cleared the Halifax airspace, and right now the plane is over international waters. The big danger point is passed. After a routine stop in Lisbon, our aircraft with its five packages will be on its way home.

"Now we have only the final implementation of Operation Deathrain. As we planned, the whole exercise has been set up and carried this far as a training sequence. Could I have a full report?''

One of the brigadiers stood and moved to a turn-over chart.

"Briefly the six planes are ready and waiting. They have been modified according to your specifications to hold the canisters. The pilots are volunteers. The targets are as we determined some time ago, the traditional targets: one canister to be sprayed over Haifa, two over Tel Aviv and Jaffa, and two set for Jerusalem.

"The actual spraying of the chemical will begin at the lowest level upwind of the target, depending on the speed of the wind. Each successive pass will be made a thousand feet higher to help the pilot avoid any of the spray. It is estimated that it will take no more than two passes of about ten miles each to empty the tanks. Colonel Farags will explain our work in developing a reliable method for opening the nozzle while airborne.''

The smallest man in the room stood. He was uncomfortable, but quickly gave a detailed explanation how the valves would be opened with the use of electrical relays and solenoids. Once they were open, there would be no way to close them. He sat down quickly, sweat showing on his forehead and on his shirt under his arms.

"Any questions?" Hassan asked.

He waited a moment and looked around the room.

"I can assure you that once the attack takes place, our ambassadors in every Arab state including Egypt will be alerted and asked to launch immediate coordinate attacks on Israel from every possible border area. Our planes will make a first strike on their airfields to knock out all their aircraft. We will, of course, use fighter protection for our spray planes. We know Israel will bring up its aircraft, but we will divert them if possible and protect our spray planes at all costs."

He looked around the room.

"My friends, this day has been centuries in coming! We have dreamed of such a strike for hundreds of years! Now it is almost within our grasp. I see no problems. When the other Arab states realize the scope, the daring, the destruction of our raids, they will cheer us and join, and together our armor will smash through the Israeli border defenses, our paratroops will land behind the lines and our combined armies will rush over them, driving all still alive into the sea like lemmings!"

The military men stood and cheered. Hassan

smiled broadly and thrust both fists over his head.

"Death to Israel!" he shouted.

"We will physically drive them into the sea!" someone else said.

The cheering went on and on. When Hassan stopped, the others did too.

"We have as our honored guest an expert in matters such as these. I would like his comments on our plans and strategy."

Everyone looked at Galkin. He rose, frowning.

"This is one of the most deadly attacks upon any people throughout history. It will work, it is brilliant, and I offer my wholehearted congratulations!" He beamed at them. "If I could give you any better methods, tactics, weapons or suggestions, I would not hesitate to do so. But I can't. I assume you have ultratight security at all points where the actual canisters are to land and be stored. I am not sure of the timing, but every *second* those canisters are on Syrian soil, they pose a horrendous danger to the Syrian people. Again, my most sincere congratulations. The moment the canisters touch ground here, they will be transferred into your hands, and the agreed-upon financial arrangements will be completed."

Hassan nodded as he thought of the financial agreement. Galkin would be rich, could do whatever he wanted to for the rest of his life. Any man can do a lot with five million U.S. dollars—twenty million Syrian pounds! He had demanded specific payments of one hundred pounds of gold in one-pound bars in twin suitcases; diamonds of four to six karats worth at least a half million dollars; and three hundred thousand dollars worth of blue-chip negotiable American stocks. The balance of some three and one-half million would be deposited the same day in a numbered Swiss bank account. Hassan had agreed quickly to the terms. The five canisters were priceless. The Syrian government had been willing to pay ten times what the Russian had demanded. He had not bargained at all. Aleksandr was a small-minded man who had small thoughts, small plans.

"Gentlemen, that ends our formal meeting. We're on schedule. If any of you has any problems or cautions, anything at all that might prove to be a delay, tell me as quickly as you can. This project, Operation Deathrain, has the highest priority of any action that this government is now engaged in. We expect nothing but total success. Thank you."

The meeting broke up. Two of the men left to check on specifics of the program. The rest talked as they stood around the big table.

Hassan motioned for the KGB man to step to the side. He spoke softly.

"You told me you had total approval from your government for our operations. Today I learned from our department of external affairs that the Soviet government has heard nothing of this plan. Why did you lie to me?"

"Choose your words carefully, Ahmed. I did not lie to you. I told you I would inform you if my government had any reservations about the plan. No one had contacted me with any objections to Operation Deathrain."

"But only because you did not tell them about it! If you did not lie to me, you deceived me. I am troubled. Have you deceived me about anything else? Are the canisters actually the same as the one that was used in El Salvador? That is a vital question you must answer immediately."

"You can answer that as well as I, Ahmed. You saw the canisters in Vancouver. You saw the lettering on the metal. You can test each canister if you wish. I have no doubts at all that they are the same as the first one."

"We will. It may hold us up a day, but we must test."

"As for my government, I have not reported in as I was supposed to. By now I have been posted as a casualty or a defector. Soon Moscow will receive notice of my tragic death in El Salvador. I was burned beyond recovery, dead and buried deep in the jungle. An unfortunate tragedy. The rebel general himself will send the telegram.

"As soon as I receive my payment for goods delivered, and after you test the canisters, I will be on my way. I think first I will stay in London. It is a free city with much to offer a person willing to pay for it, no?"

"I do not know. I live for my country. I am in the process of making history for my people!"

"And it might also vault you into the presidency, am I right, General Hassan?"

"There have been whispers. Who knows?" Hassan nodded, then held out his hand. "All right, Aleksandr. I believe you."

Voices rose from the table. The two moved back toward the others.

"I still say there is too big a price!" a voice said. "There are more than a hundred thousand Arabs living in the areas that are to be sprayed. How can we slaughter a hundred thousand of our own people!"

Aleksandr stepped forward quickly.

"My new friends, the phrase that we all must consider here is 'acceptable losses.' Say the gentleman is correct and that a hundred thousand loyal Arabs die when the gas falls. What are the enemy's losses? The death toll for the Jews could well reach *four million*! Think in percentages. Think of the lost ones as a sacrifice for victory!"

15

That night, when Bolan stepped into the dark room off the black alley in Damascus with Luana, he realized he knew little about her, and that this could all be a trap, but he was sure it was not. He sized up people quickly, and Luana was the genuine article, Mossad, field trained, deadly and fanatically dedicated.

"Fifteen," Luana said in the darkness. There was not a glimmer of light anywhere.

From the darkness came a relieved sigh of pent-up breath.

"Ah, yes, fifteen—the delightful small one, Luana. It is all right, my friends. If she comes, whoever comes with her is a friend, else he is dead."

The light came on and Bolan saw a small room in one of the older Damascus dwellings. It could have been there since 312 B.C. when Alexander of Macedonia stormed into town as the head of the fifth foreign nation to conquer Syria. Lots of stone and plaster, low lights and rugs on the floor. Six men sat around a small table. A woman scuttled out the door with a large coffeepot.

"English?" the man at the head of the table asked.

"American," Bolan said. "A guest of the management." He turned to Luana. She touched his shoulder and nodded, then sat in the empty chair and began speaking rapidly in Hebrew. Bolan felt he might as well be on an outer planet. He understood nothing she said.

Two of the men stood and began shouting at each other in German, then quieted. The heavy man who had spoken to Bolan earlier now looked up at him.

"You met General Ahmed Hassan in El Salvador? You were there at the time of the slaughter of the rebels?"

"I rode on the truck that carried the canister. I saw them blow the valve off as it rolled down a steep embankment toward the rebel camp below. I heard the cheers of the killers. Haven't you seen photographs?"

"Such photographs can be faked."

"These are not. And I believe that Syria wants to dump those canisters on Israel's biggest cities. Has there been any preparation, any secret exercises by the Syrians here during the past few weeks?"

"Several, Mr. Scott. They play at war all the time. But this is serious. They would bring deadly gas like that into the air base here. From the Western Hemisphere they usually route their planes through Lisbon for refueling. We'll get our man there and see if the Syrians expect a plane in from Canada anytime soon." He pointed at a man at the table, who quickly rose and left.

"We will notify Jerusalem at once and make contingency plans," the heavy man continued.

Bolan nodded his agreement. "It is absolutely essential to destroy or capture the canisters on the ground before they can be loaded into whatever planes the Syrians plan to use to spray the gas."

"Yes, yes. I agree," the spokesman said. He stood. "We use few names here. Call me Lucky, and you are Mack Scott. We will do everything we can. I understand you are not an official representative of your nation, not CIA or FBI. We can work with you just the same. We will have plans for the gas if it can be captured. We'd prefer that, in everyone's interest, it not be released into the air. I would not wish that even on Syria. Now we have much work to do. Thank you, Mr. Scott, for coming."

"Anything I can do, let me know." Bolan saw Luana beside him. She motioned and they went into another room, down a narrow hallway and into the street.

They took a taxi for a mile through the darkness, then left it and walked three blocks along winding streets that had been cattle paths more than three thousand years before. They slipped into the shadows of a four-story masonry building and climbed the back stairway to the second floor.

Luana opened a door, reached inside and turned on the lone electric bulb hanging from the ceiling. She looked around quickly, and he saw she had her hand in her purse. When she found no one there, she relaxed, closed the door and smiled.

"My humble home. I lived for three years in New York, and my place wasn't much better. This is my

Arab apartment. Everyone here thinks of me as an Arab. You must not be seen at the window or coming or going."

"And you don't mind my staying here?"

"Not at all." She took off her jacket and smiled. "Mr. Scott. I was in the Israeli army for two years. For the last ten months I was stationed with an intelligence unit on the border where I lived in a bunker with three men. I am not shy and they were not aggressive. It worked out fine."

"Just a thought. You are an extremely attractive woman."

"Thank you. Now I have to change and get ready to go out. I have a late date with a very important Syrian. He is the number-two man in their intelligence operation and not a careful person."

"Will you be gone all night?"

"If this takes all night, it takes all night."

Luana did not turn her back as she changed clothes. Quickly she stripped down to her bra and panties. She wore no panty hose. She began dressing in more typical Arab costume.

"There is one address you should watch," she said. "If anyone leaves, follow them. It could be nothing, and again it could be important."

She gave him the address on a piece of paper. Then she wrote her own address on another slip.

"Memorize this one—I'll help you pronounce it." She did until he had her apartment location learned. "Now don't do anything dangerous. If someone leaves that address—a man, a tall man with a heavy beard—try to follow him, but don't let him trap you."

"I've had the basic spy-tail course."

She laughed. "Good, you'll need it." She was ready. At the door she reached up and kissed his lips. It was more than a casual goodbye.

Bolan nodded. "I liked that."

"Good. See you back here as soon as I can learn what this lout knows and get away from him. He never wants me to be there in the morning."

In the street she went one way and he the other. He took a cab. The taxi stopped at the address, but Bolan asked the driver to continue down the street half a block. They were in a modern section of Damascus with sidewalks, wide streets and a few cars and buses. It could have been almost any middle-size city in the world except for the Arabic lettering on the shop signs. Bolan paid the fare, got out and faded into the shadows.

Soon he moved up two or three stores and waited again. The target of his watch was across the street, and there were lights on inside. From the window it appeared to be some kind of a tailoring or fabric store.

He pushed back into the darkness of a storefront and waited. This was the worst part. He had no weapon, not even his cane. A trio of teenage youths roamed past, obviously not following the old ways. Two of them wore blue jeans. The third had on white pants and no shirt. If it was not a Muslim country, Bolan would have wagered all three were drunk.

An hour later the lights in the shop snapped off

and soon a figure emerged from the front door. A tall man with a beard locked it in three places, put the keys in his pocket, looked both ways and then began walking away from Bolan on the other side of the street.

Tailing him was child's play in the darkness, with the shadows and the wide street. Four blocks down he crossed over to Bolan's side. He looked behind him. Fifty feet away, the Executioner slid into a dark shadow and became invisible.

Twice more in the next block the bearded man in the dark clothes looked back. By then Bolan had crossed the street and was parallel with him, or perhaps six paces behind.

For a second the nightfighter lost the man, who had darted into a gaping black alley that was little more than six feet wide. Bolan could see into it from across the street. Six long, slow heartbeats and he could find no motion, then there was a shaft of yellow light as a door opened, closed. The Executioner sprinted across the street and stepped into the alley. It was another of those basement entrances. A sign on the door showed a leg of lamb roasting over a spit. This had to be another eatery.

Bolan entered without a missed step, found himself in a dimly lit restaurant. It was not a spot where he could sidle up to the bar and order a beer. Alcoholic beverages were available in most Syrian restaurants, but not as readily as in the States. A beer, maybe. Where was the big guy with the beard? A waiter type approached him. The Executioner motioned him closer.

"Mi ami?" Bolan said, holding up both hands and looking around. The waiter shook his head.

The combatman tried again with a word dredged up from his dictionary. *"Sadig,"* Bolan said and looked around. The Arab nodded and replied something. The warrior looked from one side of the eatery to the other, but did not find the tall man with the beard.

Bolan shrugged, again lifted both hands in the air and walked toward the entrance. Someone slid out of a booth and followed him. The Executioner hurried without appearing to, went through the door and into the black void of the alley. He stepped to the alley side of the door and pressed against the wall in the Stygian darkness.

A thickset man came through the doorway. He looked down the dark alley, then sensed Bolan behind him and whirled, a gleaming six-inch blade in his hand. The Executioner snaked out of his jacket and wrapped it around his left arm, protecting it, backing deeper into the alley.

The Arab laughed, lunged and backed away. Bolan offered his protected left arm to take the thrust that never came. The Arab growled, began another lunge. The nightfighter started to lift his left arm, instead chopped it savagely downward, jolting his attacker's wrist just as it shifted from a slashing motion to a forward thrust. The American heard the bone crack, and the Arab grunt with pain. The big man grabbed the Arab's injured wrist with both hands and whirled the attacker around half a turn, then slammed him into the masonry wall.

Bolan followed up quickly with a double-fisted hammer blow to the side of the Arab's neck.

The last blow knocked out his attacker and dumped him into the dust. Quickly searching the man's pockets, Bolan found an identification folder, a wad of money and a small .32 automatic. He took the ID and the gun and walked casually into the street, then caught a cab.

It was not much, but it might be a start. He got out a block from Luana's apartment, made it to the door without being seen and used the key she had given him. She was not inside. After making sure no one was in the apartment, he sat in the darkness.

The canisters. Where were they? Had Mossad traced them? How in hell do you capture five canisters of deadly nerve gas without putting everyone in jeopardy?

Bolan paced the room, then sat down to wait for Luana. She was his only link to the success of the whole mission. He knew it would be a long wait.

16

Bolan slept.

It was nearly 3:00 A.M. when a noise jarred him—
the scraping of a pick or key in the lock. He was
awake at once, the .32 automatic in his hand, the
safety off. The Executioner had fallen asleep in a
big chair near the far wall of the apartment. He
waited now. It was a key. The door handle turned
and a small figure entered, closed the door, then
turned on the light.

"Good morning, Luana."

She turned, fear on her face replaced at once by a
smile.

"You are safe. Good. We have much to talk
about. I'll make some tea. Sorry I don't have a beer
for you."

Over hot tea she told him the bad news.

"Our people in Lisbon missed sabotaging the
plane. It is now flying toward Damascus. Officials
at Lisbon did not bother the plane or its cargo. It's
an old Boeing 707 converted passenger liner. I've
talked with my people. Several operations are under
way. We are making preparations. First we will try
to capture the canisters and threaten to blow them
up at the airport if they do not give us transport out

of the country. That should work. If not we move to plan B, then C, and even a shaky D."

"You look tired."

"Sex always makes me tired. And keeping him talking is no easy job, either." She grinned. "I usually don't complain."

"When will the canisters arrive?"

She looked at her watch. "The plane was scheduled to arrive a half hour ago at the Atsi military airfield just outside town."

"Where will they hold it and guard the canisters?"

"Hangar twelve, if everything works out right. That's all I could get from my Arab friend before he passed out."

Bolan stood. "I'm going out there for a soft probe. It won't do any good for your people to hit that hangar if it's a dummy, a false lead. We've got to know."

"I'm going with you."

"No, you're almost out on your feet."

"You'll need an interpreter."

"For fighting and making love you don't need to know the language." He showed her the .32 automatic. "I borrowed this from a friend in the alley. I followed the tall man to a small eatery. I have the address. I went in and he was gone. A man tried to kill me. He missed. I didn't. Here's his ID. Mean anything?"

She smiled as she saw the name. "A short, heavy man?"

"Yes."

"Good. I know the man and the place. I must get back to our people about this. It will help."

Bolan changed into his nightfighter blacksuit as Luana watched. Things have a way of balancing out. He had the .32 but only seven shots. He should not need that many. They both rode a taxi to his hotel, where he retrieved his cane. Then he dropped her at a small building near the one where they had been before. She told the driver where to take him.

The Executioner paid the driver and got out a block from the lighted and fenced border of the Atsi military airfield. He walked a half mile along the road next to the fence and soon found a hole through which the enlisted men had been sneaking out of camp at night.

Bolan darkened his hands and face with dirt and went through. He soon found hangar four. Well before he worked along the row to number twelve he saw it ahead. It was bathed in floodlights, special ones of every size and description.

A mounted jeep-type patrol circled the building, which faced the runway but was isolated from the others. Bolan bellied up to the edge of the darkness where it came closest to the hangar and watched the guards. There were six on the two sides he could see. Five walked given beats, and the sixth was probably a sergeant keeping tabs on the others.

Two hours until daylight. Plenty of time. Bolan worked around to the other side of the dark splotch where he could see the third side of the building. The darkness came to within ten feet of the hangar, and one guard moved in and out of the area.

Five minutes later the Executioner blended into the shadows where the guard made his deepest penetration. A small building stood close by with electrical wires coming from it to a pole. Bolan froze at the side and as the guard moved up, the cane with the fishing line snaked out, the loop dropping over the guard's head. The combatman jerked the loop tight and lunged backward, dragging the choking guard with him, the thin monofilament line slicing into neck tissue as the guard struggled.

Bolan pulled harder on the cane, and the line bit deeper; gurgles and wheezing came from the guard. Another hard lunge backward with the cane and it was over. The line had cut through flesh and one carotid artery. The Syrian died in seven seconds, his life's fluid pumped into the sandy soil.

The Executioner pulled the noose free, dragged the body behind the small building and retrieved the guard's AK-47 with its 30-round magazine. He found another magazine in the dead soldier's pocket and slipped it in his belt. Bolan bellied down in the dirt and checked the other guards. All were at the end of their assigned posts. He surged through the darkness, cane in one hand, rifle in the other. No alarm sounded as he slanted across ten feet of shadowed light to the small side door of the huge hangar.

He opened it cautiously, saw the inside was dark, and stepped through. He could make out two small planes parked to one side, and in the center a 707 with the Syrian national seal on the side. Armed men stood shoulder to shoulder around the aircraft.

Someone barked an order at the far door and half the men around the plane double-timed in formation outside. The other men spread out. There was no chance to get near the plane, let alone to get on board. He could take out a dozen of the troopers with the Russian automatic rifle, but if he did he might not get out. A soft probe was a soft probe.

Bolan turned to find a grinning guard pointing a pistol at his belly.

The man growled something the Executioner did not understand. Bolan shrugged as if in surrender, slung the rifle over his shoulder, put the cane tip to the ground and shuffled meekly toward the soldier, who had officer bars on his shoulders. The officer frowned, but watched in surprise. He said something else and Bolan lifted the cane, then quickly flipped the loop of nylon around the Syrian's arm and jerked the cane viciously. The noose tightened, slicing into the wrist, jolting the pistol from the officer's hand.

Dropping the cane, Bolan leaped forward, smashing the butt of the AK-47 into the Syrian's chin. The force of the blow jolted his head up and back and the Executioner heard his neck snap, then the man crumpled on the floor. The nightfighter pulled the noose free from the corpse's wrist and checked around. There was no one near, no one who could have heard.

He ran lightly to the same door he had come in, the AK-47 on automatic as he made for the exit. If he were lucky the dead guard outside would not have been noticed yet.

His luck had run out.

Directly opposite the outside door were two men, one looking behind the building where the dead guard lay, the other holding a rifle at the ready, peering intently into the darkness. There was no way around them. Bolan cut down both men with one 5-round burst from the stuttering Kalashnikov. He was moving before the bodies hit the ground. The Executioner grabbed the first soldier and dragged him deeper into the shadows.

A burst of gunfire tore jagged angry holes in the silent night. Someone yelled. A pistol barked twice, then the chatter of the AK-47s came. He saw the flashes ahead along the hangar. His left arm jerked and spun him around. He was hit. The force of the round dropped him into the dust. He tested his left arm. He could still move it—nothing broken. It was time to move fast.

Quickly he stripped the green fatigue shirt from the soldier he had just killed and put it on, quickly fastening every other button. Then he donned the dead soldier's soft green cap. His arm bled and throbbed, but he had no time for it now. Bleeding to death would be slower than being ripped to shreds by AK-47 spitfire.

He ran forward in the darkness. Someone challenged him and he pointed behind him, screamed, and continued forward. Three more soldiers approached him. He pointed behind him and gave the infantryman's classic signal to advance.

Then he realized the fatigue shirt he wore had captain's bars on the shoulder. He kept on moving north toward the hole in the fence. By now it might be guarded. He had no way of knowing. He saw more troops running toward the hangar.

Finally he was in the shadows again, the deep quiet of the early-morning darkness. Now he could run at his usual steady pace of seven minutes to the mile.

When he was sure he was out of the combat zone, Bolan cut the right sleeve off his fatigue shirt with his pocketknife, tore it into strips and tied it around his left arm just above the elbow where the slug had churned through flesh and muscle. It hurt like hell.

He found the hole in the fence and went through, still wearing the officer's shirt and hat. They might come in handy. He slung the rifle upside down with the muzzle pointing at the ground, pushed on the safety and walked away from the air base at a steady right angle. It was almost daylight before he found a taxi. He did not signal it. He stood in front of it with his rifle at port arms and the cabby came to a stop. Bolan opened the door and slid inside.

Three blocks from Luana's place, Bolan got out and didn't offer to pay the driver, just motioned him forward. When the taxi was out of sight, Bolan walked with the AK-47 rifle near his leg. It was still dark. He went through an alley until he found the back stairs up to Luana's apartment. She was there, waiting for him.

She saw his wound and began working on it at once. No hysterics. As she cut off the bindings and then stripped off his shirt, she asked him what happened.

He told her quickly.

She poured some disinfectant over his wound and watched him suck in his breath.

"You're tough," she said, a touch of admiration sneaking in. "I've seen bloodied troopers scream for five minutes when I did that." She shook some powder on the wound on both sides of his arm. "Looks like it nicked the bone in there. We've got to get you to a doctor."

"No time. Later. I'm good for another seventy-two hours before I pass out. I need those seventy-two."

"We'll see." She put something else on the wounds, then bandaged his arm tightly. "Yes, I know it's tight. I want it that way. Next time it will be more comfortable."

"What is your team doing?" Bolan asked.

"We're in motion. Mossad has given us A-1 priority and all the help we can find. We're on schedule. The Syrians will move the plane or the canisters now. We'll have to find out where."

"Fortunes of war."

"Fortunes of war," she repeated. Suddenly she reached out and kissed his lips softly. She pulled away.

"You need sleep," she said. "Come on."

In the bedroom she began undressing. He looked at her.

"We're going to sleep, soldier, not mess around." She took off her blouse and the long skirt and slid under the covers in her bra and panties.

Bolan took off his shirt and pants and saw that Luana was sleeping before he touched the bed. He programmed himself to wake up at eight o'clock. He closed his eyes and was sleeping almost at once.

17

When Bolan woke up he smelled hash browns and eggs. He grinned but when he tried to sit up, he got so dizzy he slumped back on the bed.

He must have groaned because Luana was at his side before he opened his eyes.

She put her hand on his forehead.

"Damn, at least 102. I'll have the doctor come and give you something. We don't want to lose you to blood poisoning."

He shook his head and tried to sit again. The whole world flipped and he let her ease him down gently on the pillow.

"We have a good doctor who works with us. He won't report the bullet wound and he has penicillin and all the good stuff."

Bolan nodded, feeling as if someone had kicked him in the head. It was nearly five minutes before his brain cleared, and then he felt as if he was burning up. Why all this from one simple gunshot wound?

She brought in the tray and put it down, then helped him ease to a half-sitting position. Her telephone rang. She picked it up. "Yes?" She listened. A moment later, saying that she understood, she put down the phone. The Israeli agent stood at the side of the bed and watched him eating.

"At least your appetite is good. I have to leave in twenty minutes. Some new developments. The doctor is to come at ten. It is arranged. I'll leave the door unlocked. He will lock it when he leaves."

Luana looked at him. He nodded. She took his face in both hands.

"You must stay in bed until the penicillin can get to work, do you understand?" He nodded. "Some of the Syrian military have been experimenting with poison-impregnated bullets. If they lodge in the target, death is the result after as little as four hours. If the bullet is removed or goes through, as with you, there can be a high-grade fever that puts the casualty down and keeps him down for as much as a week. So don't let this attack come as a shock to your macho nature. It's more than a simple wound."

Bolan heard and nodded. He was not sure he could talk.

"Thanks," he said.

She kissed his cheek and went into the kitchen. Bolan ate the rest of the breakfast and half a banana.

When Luana came back five minutes later, she had on a different outfit, a divided skirt of dark green and a military-style shirt with three creases in back. She wore a small dark hat and over the shirt, a dark green blazer.

"I'm going to meet General Quannut. He's extremely excited, says he must show me an experiment they are doing today at the air base. Some kind of a test. He insisted. But I should be back by two this afternoon.'' She stopped and watched him. "You will stay in bed?''

Bolan nodded.

He could not move if he wanted to.

LUANA HAD NEVER SEEN such a large gathering on the Atsi air base before. She had attended three or four of these exhibitions. One had been a machine-gun firing, another to demonstrate some new explosive. It was one way Abdul liked to show off. She sat beside him in the huge hangar. Everyone had been carefully cleared by guards at the door. They had simply saluted when General Quannut came through with her.

Several demonstrations had already taken place, showing the advanced capability of new shoulder-mounted rockets and launchers. Then workers wheeled in a clear, heavy plastic box with white mice in it and another with a mongrel dog inside.

General Ahmed Hassan rose and conducted the last demonstration himself.

"Ladies and gentlemen, we are now in the final stages of perfecting biological and chemical warfare testing of some new weapons. These, naturally, would be used only in retaliation if the United States or Israel uses chemicals on us first.

"However, we must have the ability to return attack for attack, which will prevent the use of such gases as it did during World War II. Now please observe the white mice cavorting in the first container. The technician will open a valve and inject a small portion of an invisible, odorless and tasteless gas. When he drops his hand the gas will be released. He will count down the seconds it takes for the mice to die. Let's watch.''

"I think I want to leave," Luana said to General Quannut to help preserve her woman's image.

"Hush, and watch. Learn something," Quannut said.

The technician lowered his hand and counted the seconds.

"One, two, three, four...." He stopped. Every mouse in the container had fallen dead.

"Four seconds!" General Hassan shouted. "Did you see that? There can be no cure for a sickness that reduces its victims into corpses that quickly. But what about on a larger animal? The dog is a mongrel from the streets. It weighs about sixty pounds. We'll use the same procedure here."

Again the man in the white lab coat lowered his hand and began to count. This time he got to nine before the dog shuddered its last and was dead.

Luana did not need to pretend. She pushed her face against the general's shoulder and would not look. He laughed at her and they made their way out of the demonstration hangar.

"We may have some news that I can tell you soon," General Quannut said. "Important news. I may even get my second star!"

She beamed at him and then pointed at another hangar.

"Why are all the soldiers standing around that

building? What's so valuable in there, our president?''

The general laughed. "Much more valuable than any politician. Yes, far more precious. In there may be the weapon that wins the war for us against Israel. We may never have to worry about the Jewish state again!''

"It's never bothered me much. Except when the war takes you away. It's going to be soon, I'll bet.''

He laughed and shook his head. "I can't even tell you that. Now I will send you home in a taxi. I have much work to get done before tomorrow morning. On your way.'' He turned and walked away without a backward glance at her. She almost stuck her tongue out at him, but knew others were watching.

Quickly she caught a taxi and got out near her apartment. By the time she unlocked the door, it was almost two in the afternoon.

"It's all right, I live here," Luana said when she unlocked the door. "Don't shoot.''

"I'm not going to shoot," Bolan said from a chair in the big room.

"You are supposed to stay in bed.''

"Doctor said I could move around a little, that it might help get rid of the toxin in my bloodstream. He gave me three shots with his biggest square needle.''

"That was the job I wanted," she teased him. She watched him a moment more. He was recovering quickly, but he would not be ready by morning. No! He *had* to be ready. She told him about the tests she had witnessed.

Bolan tried to get up. He slumped back in the chair.

"Tonight I will help you walk. You need to rest, to sleep. I'll help get you back to bed."

Bolan nodded. He had to be ready by morning. Early morning, when Mossad would make the attack. He had to be fit to fight by 2:00 A.M.! Just twelve hours away!

As he lay in her bed, Bolan heard Luana on the phone. Afterward she appeared at the door with her small hat on.

"A final meeting. Some times, coordination. Can't risk it on the phone. I'll be gone no more than an hour. You rest." She bent close and watched his eyes and brushed her lips over his cheek. "Go to sleep. After this is all over I'll take a leave and show you a nice, peaceful little place down by Jaffa. There are no crowds and the water is warm."

"Deal," he said.

She went out and he watched where she had been. Luana was becoming more than just a nurse and a friend. Bolan shook his head. He didn't need that kind of complication. Women he cared for always died. He turned his head the other way and closed his eyes.

His mission, his calling, his duty. He had to remember them. They were primary.

Bolan remembered the days when he was working closely with the U.S. government and Stony Man Farm. The team operation had given him the first real friends he had had in years, but it also brought complications.

Now he was strictly on his own, waging the war the way he knew it must be fought.

Now he functioned outside the law. That had never bothered him. Despite many scrapes with lawmen in many nations, he had never once fired a shot or taken offensive action against a lawful policeman or detective in any country. He never would.

In his personal journal Bolan had once written: "I am not above the law. In the final analysis, justice under the law is the only sure hope for mankind. But sometimes a man just can't do it by the book. Sometimes the law's own principles are in conflict with its highest ideals."

The Executioner had always said that the world was a jungle, where the first law had always been and always would be self-survival. He now knew that his decision to carry on the fight alone came from this basic jungle law. He was an excellent jungle fighter in every meaning of the word. He was a man who could take care of himself and wipe out his enemies at the same time. His skill came from long years of practice and the high development of his survival and combat instincts. He was what commanders called a "natural" fighter, using instinctively what other men had to develop slowly.

He knew his one-man war had changed him. He was not as trusting as the average man. Anyone at any time might be an enemy. He had thousands of them going all the way back to the Mafia; now added to the list were the intelligence agencies of the world and a Russian general. It simply was not practical for him to trust implicitly every man or woman he met. He took that second and third look at every offered hand of friendship, every gesture of kindness, looking for the bomb, the booby trap, the death-dealing double cross.

Sometimes he felt like a jungle panther on a tree limb, his long tail flicking in nervous agitation, making up his mind whether to leap off and make the kill.

Often in the night he stared at the darkness and wondered how much one man could accomplish. Always he had to harden his gut, freeze his human instincts and be ready and willing to wade knee-deep through enemy blood. He had the talent, the tools, the intelligence. All he had to do was apply them right up past the red danger line of survival and he could accomplish a great deal.

He did not battle the KGB for fame or fortune or glory. He wanted no newspaper headlines, TV interviews, no movies made of his life.

He demanded only a taste of justice.

Bolan sighed and tried to sit up straighter in the chair in the small apartment in the middle of Damascus, Syria. He would have his body functioning in six hours. He must! He had a call to duty! By 2:00 A.M. tomorrow he must be in fighting trim, even if he had to fool his body to do so.

He would draw from his knowledge of the fakir and from the early American Indian Dog Soldier, both of whom knew how to use the mind to overcome physical disabilities or injury. The mind can force the body to function even though it is ill or hurt. The mind can block out pain—for a while. Then, when the surging emotion and mind power finished the mission, the pain would slam back tenfold. But then the body would have the time to rest and heal completely.

Bolan thought of the Cheyenne Dog Soldiers, and drew from their understanding and their strength. When the call for action came, his mind would have his body ready.

18

Soft humming from the kitchen penetrated into the bedroom where Bolan lay, bringing him gently out of his slumber. He had slept deep. It was just before six in the evening. Slowly he sat up.

He looked around. His eyes were working normally. He felt less fevered. Bolan wore only his shorts. He pushed his feet toward the side of the bed and made it. His feet touched the floor and for a moment the room tilted, then came steady.

"Spy lady," Bolan called.

She was in the room at once, eyes bright.

"You should get into your pants." She picked them up from a chair and handed them to him.

It took two minutes to get his pants on. Then she gave him his shirt. That was easier.

Luana helped a little as he walked slowly, carefully, to the small kitchen and sank into a chair. He was applying all his mind control, fighting back the nausea. Only a desperate effort kept him moving to the chair. Before he sat down he paused. Control, dammit! He would have to think through each movement for a while.

"How did the final briefing go?" he asked her.

"Smooth. Too smooth, that worries me. I'll fill

you in after dinner. We make our first hit on the airport at 4:00 A.M."

"I'll be ready."

She looked at him as she turned the steak. "Mack, how can you be ready? You can barely stand up. I won't allow you to be in that much danger if you're not up to it. It would be a waste."

"By tomorrow morning I'll be running a hundred-yard dash in 10.5. Want to race me?"

"First we walk...."

"I'll be walking half the night, and running. I've got a few mystical tricks your fakirs might envy."

"Such as?"

"You've heard of men in combat who get so hyped up that they can be wounded and never realize it? One man led the charge and won the battle, not even knowing that his right arm was gone."

"Yes, I've heard."

"Mind over matter. I can shut out pain for several hours, isolate it, ignore it. I'll be ready."

He consumed the steak and three cups of coffee.

"You must be getting better," she said.

"Do you have a diagram of the airfield? Strong points, targets? Do we know if the gas is still in hangar twelve?"

"Our strategy is all worked out. We will have more than sixty men in the operation. Our latest information is that the canisters have been transferred to one big truck and are under heavy guard in a special area. Just before flight time the truck will drive to each of the four jets and they will load the canisters."

"We know where the truck is?"

"Yes. At the far end of the field between earth shields."

"Timing?" Bolan asked.

"Load-up time is set to begin at 0430 hours. Our strike is set for 0355 hours, while the truck is still at the far end of the field."

"I'm going after the truck. Who is on that detail?"

"Me and nineteen others. We'll all be armed with automatic rifles and four grenades each."

"Good. You're ready. Thorough, detailed, brilliant Israeli planning as usual. Let's go for a walk."

"A walk! You can hardly stand up."

"Around the apartment, until it gets dark, then up and down the stairs a dozen times and a two-mile hike down the street and back."

"You'll never make it."

"I will. We will. Then back here and another steak, not quite so well done as the last one. Then a four-mile jaunt. By morning I have to be in fighting trim."

On the first trip around the living room, Bolan was tortoiselike. He growled as he walked, first leaning on Luana, then fighting down the empty chalkiness in his gut and his backbone that seemingly had turned into jelly. He ordered his body to perform, to move, to function normally, and gradually it responded. One after another part of his body was willed into action, and soon he could walk naturally.

"Let's try the stairs," he said. Again it was a battle as the up and down movement of his legs and the strain on his lower back left bile in his throat. He fought against failure, forced his body to respond, forced his mind to direct uncooperating muscle groups to function.

They went up and down ten times, then he rested, leaning against the wall. He was glad it was dark so no one could see him.

The first block down the street went slowly. Little by little he psyched himself up into moving faster, with longer strides. It was the longest two miles of his life.

The second steak was barely warm, and he tore it apart with a steak knife and his teeth. He ate the blood-red meat like a starved man and had two more cups of coffee.

His second march down the dark streets was faster. Luana had to hurry to keep up. By the time they got home he was tired but satisfied. She gave him one more shot of the penicillin the doctor had left in the refrigerator.

"I'll sleep again, and get up at 2:00 A.M.," he told her. "Set your own alarm clock, I won't need one." He gave her a snappy salute and went into the living room and lay down on the couch.

Luana stared at him in wonder, then went to the bedroom and stretched out on the bed in her clothes. She would not undress. In the army you never undressed when on the frontier and on duty. It just was never done. She slept.

IT WAS STILL DARK as four Israeli operatives left a car near the south end of the Atsi air base near Damascus and ran quietly and unseen to a building fifty yards from the edge of the large airfield. Each man had a Russian-made, shoulder-mounted rocket launcher and five rounds. The eighteen-inch rockets were marked HE for high explosive. Two men scurried around the building, through the alley and up on the other side so they could spread their attack.

Precisely at 0355 hours one man shouldered his weapon, made sure it was loaded properly and sighted it on a military truck sitting just across the fence less than a hundred yards away. He fired. The rocket hit the cab of the truck and detonated, engulfing the rig in instantaneous fire as the fuel tank burst and added to the spreading flames.

The soldier moved six feet to one side and the second man at the corner sighted a Syrian jet fighter, three hundred yards down the runway, going through a check preparatory to a night flight. The second rocket sheared off the jet fighter's left wing, and the wing fuel tank blossomed into a roaring hell.

Four more rockets were fired in brisk, military manner, turning two more fighters, one truck and the landing light control station at the end of the runway into charred, flaming ruins. One round punched into the chain link and combat barbed wire at the edge of the airport, blasting a tank wide hole through it.

With long-practiced perfection, the four gunners launched the rest of their rounds, pulverizing the end of the runway, targeting everything they could find on that part of the field until they had only one rocket left. The main diversion had been launched.

Sirens whined, combat troops advanced from the north toward the sudden explosions at the south perimeter, moving cautiously as the last rounds hit, then rushing to the hole in the fence and charging through. Just as fifteen Syrian army men were crowding through the gap, the last Israeli in the team used his final round and blew the soldiers straight into the hands of Allah.

At precisely 0350 at the main gate of the big air base, a pickup truck stalled. The driver got out and kicked the fender, talked to the sergeant and private on duty at the gate and said he would be right back with jumper cables. The two men volunteered to push the light pickup out of the lane of traffic that was backing up as early arrivals started coming to the base.

When the driver was two hundred yards from his truck, he took a small red box from his pocket, snapped a switch and looked at his wristwatch. When the minute hand showed the time was exactly 0355, he pushed the red button.

A hundred pounds of plastic explosive in the pickup detonated, shattering the gate, vaporizing the two soldiers pushing the rig and setting on fire twelve cars and trucks in the waiting line.

More sirens wailed.

Far across the airport near the officers' quarters, a pickup pulled to a stop outside the high fence. One man jerked a tarp off a fifty-caliber machine gun mounted in the truck box. A second man jumped in to guide the ammunition belt. The second the gunner heard the rockets exploding at the south end of the air base, he raked the barracks and any moving thing with fifty-caliber machine-gun fire.

Four men pushed their heads out the barracks windows. Three of them became statistics as the heavy rounds thundered into their bodies, slamming them back into their rooms. Six men rushed from the near door in skivvies and white T-shirts, making them perfect targets in the glow of the porch light.

All six danced as the fifty-caliber lead messengers punched them into Allah's palace.

A military-police jeep careered around a corner toward the sound. The Israeli gunner shattered the windshield, decapitated the driver and killed the passenger, then riddled the crashed jeep. It burst into fire from spilled gasoline.

The fifty-caliber machine gun chattered out death for seven minutes until the three boxes of ammunition were gone, then the driver powered away. His crew had not taken a single round of return fire.

At the north side of the field, near the area's massive ammunition-dump bunkers, Bolan, Luana and twenty heavily armed Israeli commandos hovered in a drainage ditch outside the fence. Two sappers had wired the fence and were ready to blow a gaping hole in it on signal. The bunkers were thirty feet wide and a hundred feet long, covered with ten feet of packed earth.

Their watches showed 0355 hours. Then the rockets exploded to the south, and a moment later they heard machine-gun fire.

The chain link fence in front of them erupted in flame and smoke as a jolting shock preceded the sound of the explosion. The fence had an opening six feet wide and the commandos bolted through it in combat order, advancing toward the center of the mounds, where the truck holding the canisters was supposed to be parked.

Rifle fire snarled in front of them. The troops hit the dirt. The commander, a captain, sent four men around the closest mound and put a light machine-gun team on top of it.

Bolan ran up the slope with the machine gunners. They had a small bipod-mounted machine gun that fired 7.62mm slugs and could chatter away all day with just one man handling it. The second man carried belted ammunition. Bolan knew the gun could kick out over five hundred rounds a minute.

On top of that mound they had a clear view of the next three and could more easily spot defenders. Quietly they set up with the gunner prone behind the weapon. They killed three Syrians in ten seconds. Near one mound they could see the top of the tractor trailer that contained the gas cylinders.

They covered the advance of the main body, then leapfrogged ahead. Newly dug trenches surrounded the big truck. Spaced, defensive fire came from the trenches. An Israeli soldier beside Bolan took a round through the throat and fell, bleeding to death. Three more Israeli attackers were cut down when a machine gun opened up from under the truck.

Luana had been on the other side of Bolan, firing to keep down the gunners in the trenches as their men moved ahead. Now she passed Bolan two grenades.

"Roll them into the trenches," she said.

Bolan pulled a pin on the first one and threw it overhand toward the holes a hundred feet ahead of them. The smooth bomb hit on the dirt, rolled to the left, then straight ahead and vanished into the trench. There was an agonized scream just as the bomb detonated. Bolan threw the second grenade, another hit, then used his AK-47 to riddle the front tire on the big tractor. As the thirty slugs slammed into the tire, it hissed and the rest of the air gushed out as the front of the heavy-duty tractor sagged to one side.

Bolan heard a new surge of firing. It came from what sounded like a company of infantry troops to the south. A few small knee mortar rounds began falling near the Israelis.

The Executioner crawled on hands and knees to the next ammo bunker mound where he saw Luana. She was dressed in camouflaged fatigues as were the rest of the attackers, and her AK-47 was hot from firing.

"Do we have any radio?" Bolan asked her.

She turned her face, which was streaked with patterns of dirt, and nodded. "We use it only if we have to."

"We've got at least a company out there with

machine guns and mortars. They'll cut us into pig food.''

As he spoke he heard more explosions on the field. A Syrian jet began to take off just as a shoulder-fired missile hit it. The erupting jet fuel tanks and missiles under the wings roared for almost a minute.

"Is there going to be any Israeli air?" Bolan asked.

She nodded.

"We could use some help with that bunch to the south. Do we have any marker flares?"

Luana brought up a handy-talky-type radio and punched the send button.

"Bumblebee, this is Attila," she said in Hebrew. "Request close support, near truck at north end of field. Will mark with red flare. Soonest!"

She told him what she asked for. Bolan took the red flare and fired it into the section where the company-sized Syrian army troops continued to advance.

"I'm going to the top of this next bunker mound," the combatman said.

"I'm coming with you." The look in her eye told him not to protest. He knew she could take care of herself.

They edged up to the top of the dirt mound and looked over. From the thirty-foot height they could see more of the situation.

The truck would not be able to move out to supply the five Syrian jets with the canisters. The flat front tire had taken care of that. But the Syrians were starting to fan out, to encircle the area.

Before others than scouts could move, Israeli jets rocketed not more than fifty feet above the air base. They were American-made F-4 Phantom jets with Israeli markings. One did a tight turn of about three miles and came back. Six wing rockets thundered into the spot where the red flare still burned. One 60mm mortar and crew disintegrated in a direct hit. A machine-gun crew was blown away from its weapon by shrapnel and dumped into a trench.

"Thanks, Bumblebee. Find a new target. Attila is happy."

She told him what she had said in Hebrew, and Bolan grinned as he kept his AK-47 busy harassing the retreating troops. It was nearly dawn. They could see marginally through the dusky light.

"They'll be back with help," Luana said, "unless this was a dummy truck."

To the south more Israeli jets slammed rockets and bombs into the military buildings, barracks and planes on the ground. Bolan could see half a dozen Syrian jet aircraft on the ground burning. The surprise had been total.

Two Syrian half-tracks, with heavy machine guns chattering, rolled into view around ammo bunkers farther down the field. They riddled the tops of the bunkers where the small Israeli force lay.

"Stay down!" Bolan shouted, and someone repeated the warning in Hebrew. Before Luana had time to summon the Israeli air, one of the Phantoms lashed out of the sky and caught a half-track with a direct hit, exploding ammunition inside and rolling it over twice, leaving it lying on its top, burning fiercely. The second half-track scurried behind another ammunition mound.

The Israelis moved forward until they were on two sides of the big truck trailer that held the canisters. It was now only a mopping-up exercise as the disciplined attackers moved with caution and skill, clearing the mounds and their entrances, which were locked.

Bolan and Luana stared over the earth mound at the Utility trade-name label on the aluminum trailer.

"Cover me," Bolan said. "I've got to make sure this is the right trailer."

19

Bolan felt hot lead bite his thigh. Only a scratch. He dived behind the big truck and was out of sight of the defenders. The big handle was held in place by a heavy padlock. The Executioner backed off and put a burst of parabellums into it, shattering the hasp. He flipped the handle and swung open the door that took up half the opening.

Inside he saw the five sleek canisters. They were spread over the floor of the forty-foot trailer, each carefully braced and padded for a quick move. It would take a forklift to unload them. The Executioner backed out and closed the door, fastening a bolt through the remainder of the big hasp.

The Israeli jets slammed overhead again, one gunning the remainder of the company that had been defending the trailer. While the troops were occupied, Bolan sprinted back up the slope of the ammo bunker and slid over the top.

"That's the real thing down there."

Luana nodded, and below Bolan saw a final Israeli assault on the trenches. It came after twenty grenades had exploded in the slits. Sixteen Israeli commandos surged from behind the humps of earth and charged the trenches. There was one brief flurry of answering fire that ended with a scream.

Bolan motioned and they ran down the slope and into the trenches a dozen feet in front of the tractor. As they jumped into the four-foot hole, one Syrian, only wounded, raised a rifle, his finger on the trigger.

Luana was faster, slamming a 5-round burst from her Kalashnikov into his chest. She jumped forward, kicked the rifle from his dying hands. Bolan watched her and when she was sure the man was dead, she looked at him. He nodded grimly and they checked the others, making sure all were dead. They gathered the rifles and stood the extras beside each man in the trenches. Some of the Syrian bodies were thrown out of the trenches to the rear.

"We can't drive that rig out of here. How do you figure to get the canisters to Israel?"

"The plan is to airlift them if we make the right connections." She picked up the radio.

"Big Bird, the area is secure. I repeat, the area is secure. Can Big Bird fly? This is Attila."

The radio sputtered, then came to life. "That's a negative, Attila. We have hornets still active. Will advise."

Two more Israeli Phantom jets thundered overhead, but did not fire. They climbed in a graceful arc and headed southwest.

"Is that the quickest way to Israeli territory?" Bolan asked.

Luana nodded. "How far do you think it is?"

"Three hundred miles?"

She laughed. "We're in the Middle East now, not

the plains of Texas. Actually it's a little less than fifty miles to Metulla, a little village in the finger of Israel that juts into Syria and Lebanon. We need a fifty-mile air corridor free of Syrian jets before we move."

"Trouble!" the Executioner said. He had been watching south and now saw the half-track that had earlier retreated nose around an ammo bunker five hundred yards away and turn toward them. The heavy machine gun chattered and Bolan ducked. The rounds dug into the dirt and Syrian corpses on each side of the truck, but none hit the trailer.

"Wish we had about three LAWs," Bolan said. "Where are those friendly jets? This guy can wade right over us."

"Some of that good Israeli planning," Luana said with a wry grin. "The trouble is we should have brought one of the shoulder rocket launchers with us."

She tried the radio again, but got no immediate response from Bumblebee. The half-track ground closer, and Bolan could see Syrian soldiers crowding behind the protection of the mechanical fort.

"Flank him," Bolan said. "Get me four men and a machine gun. Plenty of ammo at this end of the trench. Fast!"

She ran down the trench bent over, calling out orders.

Exactly three minutes later Bolan and his team waited for the covering fire from the troops in the trenches, then went over the top and stormed toward the nearest ammo bunker to the left. They had forty yards to go and spread out so no lucky burst could get more than one. One man groaned and went down halfway to safety. The others charged ahead.

One of the Israelis looked back. Bolan barked at him as they ran around the bunker and raced down two earthen humps, then another, falling into position behind an underground storage area. They heard the half-track coming abreast of them, rushed up the back of the slope to the front, set up the machine gun and went prone.

Bolan told them not to fire before he did. They could see the half-track pulling past them, thirty yards away, with twenty Syrians crowding the safety alley behind the armored rig.

When the infantry were past and the vulnerable back of the half-track was exposed, Bolan nodded.

"Now!" he said and put a burst into the cab of the half-track. Each man had a target: two on the infantrymen, the machine gun and Bolan on the half-track.

Their first salvo cut down ten men, but Bolan saw thirty or forty rounds punch into the cab of the half-track without effect. They moved their firepower to the side of the motor area and fired burst after burst until the engine belched smoke and the rig slowed to a stop. Then the motor sputtered, started, stopped, started and gunned, and the half-track moved ahead again at half speed.

As the half-track coughed, the ambushers concentrated on the men behind it, who now raced for cover. None made it.

The four on the ammo bunker earth mound fired

at the lumbering half-track. No one was on the outer heavy machine gun. Bolan lifted the grenades that remained on his belt. He waved the men with him.

"Grenades!" he said. They ran around two of the ammo mounds and came up even with the slowly moving rig.

All four charged the side of the machine. There was no firepower there. At twenty yards they threw the bombs and hit the dirt. Two landed short, one hit the rear of the rig and the last penetrated the canvas cover over the driver's compartment. All exploded.

When the shrapnel stopped flying they ran forward and threw again. This time when the four grenades went off the big machine coughed and stopped. Bolan's AK-47 blazed at the cab of the half-track until he ran out of rounds. Then another man picked up the target.

Slowly they advanced on the machine. No one was in the back. Bolan jumped up on the tracks and vaulted into the rig, his automatic rifle primed and ready. He kicked aside the tarp over the front and found two men slumped over the controls, both riddled with bullets.

A few minutes later Bolan and his team dropped back into the trenches around the trailer.

"Did you get our wounded man?" Bolan asked.

Luana looked up and nodded. "We couldn't save him."

"Sorry. How many have we lost?"

"Four dead, three wounded, not seriously."

"Where is Big Bird? We can't hold this spot all day."

"Coming. We just got clearance on the air corridor. Big Bird will be here in four minutes."

"How do we load them? Those canisters must weigh a ton each."

"We don't unload them, Mack. You'll see."

A friendly jet came at them from the north like a speck in the sky and flashed over them before they heard the sound.

"We own the air, at least for a while. We need to control it for another hour."

"But it takes a jet about three minutes to go sixty miles. If it's traveling at 1,200 miles an hour, that's what—twenty miles a minute?"

"Our bird won't move quite that fast."

A minute later he understood. A huge CH-54 Tarhe Sky Crane throbbed into sight. The rig looked like a flying skeleton with a cabin on the front and a long skinny framework body under a big rotor where 105 howitzers, trucks or shipping containers could be picked up and flown away.

"Beautiful!" Bolan said. "Let's get that tractor unhooked from the fifth wheel." Two men helped detach the tractor and crank down the front legs of the trailer so they supported the front half of its weight. Then they pushed the tractor forward until the fifth wheel connection was free.

By then the big chopper hovered overhead and tiedown slings were lowered. They were reinforced by chains. A specialist descended a rope ladder and supervised.

Down the field Bolan saw dust from two vehicles coming toward them. "Half-tracks," he said. He grabbed the machine gunner. "Can you work that heavy MG down there on that dead half-track?"

"Yes."

"Let's go." He looked at Luana. "You get out of here on this chopper. You're blown now. Nobody in Damascus will trust you again."

She nodded and he ran.

They got to the half-track and primed the heavy gun. It had been hit by rifle fire but was undamaged. In the rig they found two boxes of belts of ammo. By the time they got the weapon turned around the other half-tracks were in range.

The Israeli commando chattered off a 10-round burst into the lead half-track. It spun to one side and the gunner put another ten rounds into the tracks.

The second half-track returned fire and missed. The Syrians hovered behind the crippled rig, but Bolan's team kept peppering the area around it with rounds, until the other half-track approached with the heavy MG blazing. They were still three hundred yards apart, and before the far weapon had the range, the Israeli gunner blew the Syrian half-track's tread off and it went in a circle. A final burst of rounds came from the heavy weapon. One hit Bolan's gunner in the neck and tore off his head. Another caught Bolan in the right shoulder and spun him around, dumping him off the half-track.

As nearly as he could tell, he didn't lose consciousness, but as he looked up he saw the Sky Crane lifting gently away from the ground with the trailer. Wheels and all sailed higher and higher into the air as the strange-looking chopper and its dangling cargo of deadly nerve gas turned once and headed south-west.

As it left, a smaller helicopter swung in to land. It looked like a UH-1D as used in Nam. It could hold fourteen men and a crew. Through a pinkish haze Bolan saw the dust billow as the chopper landed. Blinking, he made out figures getting inside. Four-teen. He tried to count backward. They lost four, fifteen left. Then lost one more here, fourteen, came out even. No, Luana was fifteen. Might get her on board. His mind buzzed and whirled and for a moment it was midnight dark. Then he could see again.

He shook his head, saw the bird finish loading and surge upward and slant southwest much faster than the Sky Crane. She was gone. Good. Luana must be away and safe.

Bolan looked at his shoulder. Bad. Blood all the hell over his arm and sleeves. Get back to the fence and through. Get away. Get away!

He stood and the roadway moved, then steadied. He began to walk toward the truck trailer. For several steps he sidled to the left, the way he used to when as a child he was swung around in a circle, and then tried to walk. At last the ground stopped moving.

Blood. Blood dripping down his fingers. Too much blood. He had to stop it. Damn fifty caliber smashed an arm all to hell.

Bolan sat down in the dirt and fumbled for the first-aid pouch on his web belt. He broke it open and dumped the powder over the wound. But he couldn't wrap it with one hand. He unrolled the bandage, bunched it up and pressed it into the wound.

The flood of pain made him cry out. Blood red blinded him again. The big red ball in front of his eyes faded slowly. It had blotted out his vision for thirty seconds. His sight and the world slowly came back into focus. He shook his head, looked at the dead truck tractor sitting a hundred yards ahead. It looked like a hundred miles. He stood and walked toward it.

Beat down the pain. Use mind control. Dammit, the game wasn't over yet!

Mack Bolan still held the AK-47 as he stumbled the last few yards to the trenches.

No one there.

No one alive.

Then he saw a man wave. An Israeli. The man ran up. He didn't speak English. He made motions that the others had left. Bolan nodded and sat down in the trench. The Syrians would be coming soon. A second wave would come with many rockets and tanks and machine guns.

He turned and from the other way in the trench he saw someone running toward him.

Luana!

He saw tears in her eyes as she rushed up. At once she was working on his shoulder. Tears streamed down her cheeks. She told him quickly that the chopper could hold only fourteen and the wounded took up more room, so she stayed with one man. They were about to come looking for him.

Bolan nodded. He thought he saw some movement from the south but when he blinked and looked again he saw nothing. Had it been a man running around one of the ammo bunkers or just his imagination?

Luana bandaged his shoulder, gave him a drink from her canteen.

"Easy on that, it's straight bourbon," she said, her dark eyes serious, worried.

He took two swallows of the straight whiskey and shook his head. That would do something—he wasn't sure what.

The Israeli jumped out of the trench and said something to Luana in Hebrew. A second later a burst of rifle fire rattled in the still Syrian morning air and the Israeli commando hurtled back into the trench, his chest splattered with blood from five bullet wounds. He was dead.

Luana grabbed a rifle and peered over the parapet. She frowned, seeing nothing.

"Stay down!" Bolan shouted, his voice sharp.

She looked at him and the enemy rifle spoke again, a single round that hit Luana's head and slapped her backward into the trench. Bolan stared at the woman, her eyes closed, the whole side of her head bloody.

He roared in anger and fury, grabbed his AK-47 and two extra magazines and hurried toward the point where the shots had been fired. It had been one man doing the firing, a single man. And now it was between the two of them. To fight, and to live or to die.

20

Bolan went over the top of the trench, emptying the AK's magazine in a wild rage. He stormed up the side of the nearest ammo bunker. It was on this side of the bunker where the rifleman had been. Who was the man? Why the solo attack?

The top of the bunker was a low crown so he could lie out of sight and see down the far side. No one had come around the next bunker yet. He held the high ground for the moment.

Again a wave of red spots appeared before his eyes, blinding him. He tried to will them away, mind over matter. He fought them off until he could see clearly again. It had taken thirty seconds, maybe more. His shoulder throbbed and ached but he could use it. He could command it to perform.

The enemy. Where was the enemy?

Movement! At the far end of the bunker he saw a man slip around, look at the earthen mound where Bolan lay. He did not look up.

Clear shot!

His enemy was in the open. Bolan put the rifle on full automatic and leveled in. His shoulder stabbed him with tremendous pain as he moved his arm up to hold the rifle.

He had to fight over pain.

Again he brought the sights in on the man just as he began to run forward. Bolan sprayed him with fifteen rounds. The climb of the Kalashnikov was minimal. The Executioner saw the rounds striking around the man, but he did not go down. He saw the bloody wound on the man's upper left arm.

They both were wounded.

Before Bolan could change magazines, the man vanished behind the far end of the same bunker Bolan lay on.

Bolan ran along the top of the hundred-foot mound, watching the end and the far side where he thought the Syrian might come out. The man did not show.

The Executioner flattened out at a spot where he could cover the trenches and the end of the bunker, a fresh 30-round magazine in the AK.

He waited.

For five minutes there was no movement, no sound. Then he heard explosions and rifle fire at the far end of the base. There was nothing valuable up here now, nothing to capture or defend, so the Syrians had not sent a force up here. Then why one man?

As Bolan pondered, he saw an arm and then a black ball sailing toward him through the hot dusty air.

He watched the small bomb coming. It was short and to the left. Bolan rolled away from it, the rifle clamped on his chest. As he rolled over his left shoulder he groaned in blinding pain. The red wave washed over his retinas and he could see nothing. The grenade went off with an ear-throbbing roar and he felt one shard of shrapnel hit his leg. But it was small and he was not even sure it had penetrated the skin. He could see nothing for ten seconds. Then the red curtain eased, faded, shattered into splinters and vanished after another five seconds.

First he looked at the trenches. The man was not there. The Executioner took the last grenade from his shirt pocket and pulled the pin. He threw it where he had seen the arm. The bomb hit and bounced, then rolled over the lip of the bunker and went off. He heard screams of pain.

Almost before the explosion faded, a head jolted up and looked over the mound. Bolan fired six rounds, then he heard a sound every combat man dreads—the clack of a jammed weapon. He tried to unjam it, but it would take a tool. The Executioner knew he had to get back to the trenches for another weapon.

The head bobbed up again, and this time Bolan could see the features. The man was not a Syrian.

He was Aleksandr Galkin. The Russian had come for vengeance. The Executioner ran back the way he had come, along the top of the mound, then down the far side. He carried the rifle as a bluff. It almost worked.

He was twenty feet from the trenches when a burst of hot lead churned the ground around him. All missed. He looked toward the end of the near mound and saw the Russian working on his weapon. He had run out of ammunition.

Bolan turned and ran toward him, the fury building in him. As he ran the thirty yards, he pulled an Israeli fighting knife from his belt. He saw the Russian taking out his own knife.

Aleksandr straightened when his enemy was ten yards away.

"So, it has come down to this, American?" he said.

"You and me, Galkin. No Syrians, no Russians, no Israelis and no Americans. Just two men and two knives."

"I was always good with a knife," Galkin said.

Bolan was four inches taller than the other man. Galkin was overweight and the Executioner guessed out of shape. But a sharp blade would cut for any hand.

Beside Galkin lay a briefcase. Bolan motioned to it.

"Your five million dollars?"

"Part of it. They paid on delivery, of course. How they handled the canisters after that was their problem."

"Considerate of you." Bolan saw the wound on the Russian now. It was bad, still bleeding. The left arm hung at Galkin's side, which meant nothing. He could be faking that much. "I should have taken you out in Idaho."

"You were there?"

"Remember the guard the dogs tore apart? I should have finished your safehouse that night."

Bolan moved forward, the six-inch blade held in front of him with the tip forward the way one would hold a pointer. It was the classic knife-fighting position that let you slash up, down or sideways, or drive forward in a thrusting motion.

Galkin nodded as he assumed the same pose.

"We could bargain," the Russian said. "I have almost two million American dollars in this brief-case. We could split it evenly, and each walk out of the base by a different route."

"I want it all, then I might let you go," Bolan said.

"I never know when Americans are joking. It doesn't matter, you would not accept a compromise."

"You have that right."

They were ten feet apart. Bolan held out his left arm so Galkin knew he had use of it. The Russian's left arm hung by his side.

The Executioner drove in with the blade, his boots dancing through the sand. He faked a slashing blow to the belly, stopped it and swung the sharp blade at Galkin's right shoulder. The steel caught only the tan shirt the Russian wore, making a two-inch tear.

As Bolan jumped back, he felt the throbbing pain in his shoulder from the jolt, but beat it down.

The Russian came forward slowly, as if tired. Then suddenly he charged, his left arm rising to take any blow from Bolan's knife, so he could get inside.

The Executioner slashed the left arm, sidestepped and spun away from the swinging cold steel. He suffered only a scratch on his left shoulder above the bullet wound.

Quickly they faced each other again.

"My offer still stands," Galkin said. "Half for each of us."

Bolan felt the red coming back, fought it, but knew it would flood over his eyes soon. Slowly he shook his head at the offer. The Russian stood six feet away, facing him. In ten seconds the Executioner would be helpless. He shifted his grip on the handle, and in a swift and long-practiced movement threw the heavy knife. The attack came so swiftly that Galkin had time only to lift his right arm and start to drop away.

The knife flew the six feet point first, penetrating between ribs as Galkin fell to the ground, gripping the handle of the blade.

He stared at Bolan in disbelief, then his eyes closed and opened. The blade had missed his heart, but severed two large arteries. He coughed, spit up blood.

Bolan let the red haze come then, not knowing how long it would last. He stared hard through unseeing eyes at Galkin, at the place where he had been when the mists had blocked out his sight. For fifteen seconds the Executioner stood there, blind, waiting, listening to the man in the sand. Galkin made only one sound, a rasping wheezing, then he coughed as he strangled on his own blood and fell back into the sand.

When Bolan's sight returned after twenty seconds, he saw the Russian dead on the ground, a pool of blood in the sand beside his mouth.

Bolan sagged to his knees, then stood, holding his left arm across his chest and ran back to the trench.

He looked down at the woman he thought was dead. She had just finished washing the blood off the side of her head, and had a bandage half in place.

"Sorry I got hit just when you needed me," Luana said. "It just grazed my head but bled as if I'd been slaughtered. That shoulder!"

She helped him into the trench, and he saw she had four loaded rifles and six grenades stacked beside her. "I figured the Syrians would come sooner or later."

He put his good arm around her and held her closely for a moment, then blinked and eased away.

He saw the small radio lying on top of the grenades.

"Remember that last chopper?" she said. "I just talked to some of our air. They're sending in another one. ETA is five minutes. Gives me time to get that shoulder patched up."

Bolan nodded, then looked back at where he had left the Russian KGB agent.

"First a small detour." He stepped out of the trench and walked to the spot where Aleksandr Galkin had set down his briefcase. It was worth a look. There could be some cash in the bag. He carried it back to the trench.

"Open it," he said to Luana.

She unsnapped the clasp and spread the bag top open. Bolan saw several big envelopes. Inside one he found negotiable American stocks and bonds of large denominations.

Luana opened a small blue velvet bag with drawstrings. When she looked inside her eyes went wide, then she rolled something into her hand.

In her palm lay ten brilliant-cut diamonds, each from four to six karats.

"Oh, my!"

"Each one of those stones is probably worth a hundred thousand dollars," Bolan said.

"Galkin's payoff? Was that Galkin who shot me?"

"Yes. And those baubles are your medical-insurance payment."

"Oh, I couldn't."

"We'll talk about that later. If your chopper friends get here before the Syrians do. Look down there."

They saw a dust trail lifting off the desert floor. It came from across the field and angled directly for them.

Bolan put the diamonds and stocks back in the briefcase.

They each set up four rifles on the small parapet and waited.

"Bumblebee. Calling Bumblebee. This is Little Bo Peep. Where are you? The wolf is coming."

"Peeper, glad you're still there. Our ETA is about one minute. Not to worry about that six-by truck headed your way. We'll make a run on him coming past."

They could hear the faint *whup-whup* of the chopper then. A stain in the sky wheeled and two rockets jetted from the chopper and exploded below. One caught the truck in the side and rolled it three times and set it on fire.

The chopper powered on toward them, circled the dead highway tractor and its trenches as the pilot and gunner checked for enemy troops, then settled to the ground.

"Come on, Little Bo Peep, I think you've found your sheep," the Executioner said.

21

The warm water swept ashore in a small wave, crested and rolled over the brown sand. Mack Bolan took a deep breath and let it escape slowly. The sun overhead was warm; it would soon be too hot for his kind of limited beach play. He stood slowly, washed the sand off his legs and strolled to a solitary umbrella on the mile-long stretch of deserted beach.

The Executioner sat down in the shade beside Luana, who wore a bikini and rubbed sunscreen lotion on her arms. They were on a secure beach about five miles from the small village of Ashdod in southern Israel, down toward the Gaza Strip.

Bolan winced as he sat down. Any strain on the shoulder came through loud and clear now. He and Luana had walked to the chopper that last day at the Atsi airport in Damascus and had been put on stretchers at once and treated like casualties for three days by the Israeli army medics. By the time Luana made her explanations and told "Mack Scott's" part in the plot to destroy Israel, the story had leaked to the press.

Israel had wanted to declare Mack a national hero, but he had bluffed them with talk about a top-security problem and that any such notice would blow his cover and his usefulness in future operations. He talked them into using another name for him and downgrading his part in the operation. He insisted that Luana be given a medal for her part.

The incident would soon blow over and be only a minor paragraph in the history of Israel, but the tightening up of American security should be beneficial and long lasting.

The crease along the side of Luana's head was healing. She had taken a week's leave and was nursing him like a mother hen. They were living alone in a cabin just behind the small sand dunes. The place had a view of the water, all the comforts and was directly adjacent to a highly classified and secure army zone.

They watched TV and she interpreted the newscasts for him. They watched American dramas with subtitles and he told her when the subtitles didn't quite tell the whole story.

For a week they had been wading, swimming, sunning and at night watching the stars from a bonfire on the beach.

No longer did the red tide block his vision. The medics said it was all a part of the shock he'd suffered after the wound, and it had almost killed him.

They still had the briefcase. Bolan had kept it with him and told the authorities it had top-secret material inside, which he was responsible for. They did not question his word, and even now the briefcase sat in the cottage living room.

"Have you decided about the money?" he asked her.

Luana looked away, dark eyes troubled. She turned toward him, a small frown on her face, then sighed.

"No, I haven't. True, it is Syrian money. It is not stealing to take it, to use it for good causes. But I feel it should go to the government."

He touched her hand. "Luana. I need money to finance my operations. I'll take half of it—the stock certificates. You can use the rest as you want to. Give it all to the Israeli national treasury, or start your own offensive against Syria. Or you could buy some reasonably sized diamonds and a mink coat. But promise me you'll save some of it for yourself. You earned it the hard way."

"That sounds like a good plan. You'll have enough to keep working. And I'll have some satisfaction, maybe both ways. I don't have to decide right now."

Luana reached over and touched his shoulder. "Remember in my apartment when I told you I was just another soldier?"

"Yes, I remember."

"And we slept in the same bed that night and you never touched me?"

"Yes."

"Now I feel different. I don't want you to think of me as one of the guys."

He reached out and kissed her soft lips and she responded.

"Do you want to go up to the cabin?"she murmured.

"No."

"Right here?"

"Yes. Right here, right now."

She watched him, her face serious. Then she smiled, reached out and kissed his lips again. She untied her bikini top and let it fall to the towel.

"Mack, I love you," she whispered.

DON PENDLETON'S EXECUTIONER
MACK BOLAN

Sergeant Mercy in Nam... The Executioner in the Mafia Wars... Colonel John Phoenix in the Terrorist Wars.... Now Mack Bolan fights his loneliest war! You've never read writing like this before. Faceless dogsoldiers have killed April Rose. The Executioner's one link with compassion is broken. His path is clear: by fire and maneuver, he will rack up hell in a world shock-tilted by terror. Bolan wages unsanctioned war—everywhere!

GOLD EAGLE

Available wherever paperbacks are sold.

AVAILABLE SOON!

MACK BOLAN

Resurrection Day

Could the one thing to stop Mack Bolan be his own flesh and blood? Mack's long-lost brother, Johnny, returns—with the Mafia in tow! Mack's back in his third SuperBolan.

"Millions of Americans are turning to the incomparable Mack Bolan."

Chicago Sun Times

Readers react to the explosion called BOLAN

You know that typical, getting-a-conversation-started-at-a-party question: "If you were going to be stranded for the rest of your life on a deserted island, what 10 books would you take along?" I've thought a lot about the question. I have literally hundreds of favorites. I'd take the Bible, Shakespeare and maybe *Gone With the Wind*. Then I'd cheat a little. I'd empty my suitcase (who needs clothes on a deserted island?) and fill it up with *Mack Bolan*!

—*K.H., Bostic, North Carolina*

I have read various books here and there throughout my life, but I have yet to find any that could hold my interest like the Executioner. There is something about the Executioner that makes me a loyal fan. It's hard to put into words, but what I'm trying to say is that in the Executioner books I see truth. Mack Bolan is not portrayed as a superman, yet he achieves super results in a totally believable way. I've been trying to gather all the pieces of my life into one bundle and figure out who the hell I am, and I can't explain how, but your books help me immensely. Thank you!

—*G.B., USSDD Eisenhower*

I have received my latest shipment of books from Gold Eagle, and I feel like a child on Christmas Eve. I want to thank all those involved for this exceptional reading material. We readers can almost smell the gunpowder! And *Automag** is tops. Do you remember the old Aunt Jemima TV commercial where they said "What took you so long?" That's exactly how I feel. Thanks!

—*D.B., Kilgore, Texas*

**Automag: The Magazine of Action Adventure, is available through the Gold Eagle Reader Service.*

I read my first Executioner while stationed at Fort Richardson, Alaska. The difference in quality from other adventure series was remarkable and glorious. Mack Bolan has changed my life. I now teach my four children that morals and values are more than loving thy neighbor, that we must be willing to help our neighbor in times of need. I explain news bulletins and world situations to the two older children. All this because Mack Bolan showed me that no place is safe unless you keep it safe. —*C.T., Prior, Oklahoma*

I want to compliment your outstanding Executioner series. I have just finished one, *Paramilitary Plot*, and think it is your best ever. When school started this year, I found out we had to write about our favorite book. For me, it was an easy choice. Mack Bolan is the greatest hero that has lived in the mind of any author. Believe me, there are many other students who feel this way. I hope the series will continue forever. *M.S., Cheyenne, Wyoming*

Thank you for the Executioner, the most interesting series of books. I have never liked reading but by accident one day on my way to the dentist's office, I purchased a recent book in your series and I was hooked. I just had to find out what led Mack to make such war! To my astonishment, I found I was enjoying reading. I purchased as many of the earlier books as I could get my hands on and read them in a week. I couldn't wait for the next book to come out, and I still find it hard to wait for it. —*V.B., Bowling Green, Indiana*

I am presently in the U.S. Army and served with the elite 82nd Airborne Division for a decade. The adventures of Mack Bolan have rewarded me with hours and hours of enjoyable pleasure over the years. I feel the same way about Able Team and Phoenix Force. These books' realistic description of weapons, tactics and personal capabilities is unequalled by any other publisher. Your research remains uncanny in those areas. And your books are far closer to the truth than most people realize.

—*D.H., APO, New York*

HE'S EXPLOSIVE. HE'S MACK BOLAN... AGAINST ALL ODDS

He learned his deadly skills in Vietnam...then put them to good use by destroying the Mafia in a blazing one-man war. Now **Mack Bolan** ventures further into the cold to take on his deadliest challenge yet— the KGB's worldwide terror machine.

Follow the lone warrior on his exciting new missions...and get ready for more nonstop action from his high-powered combat teams: **Able Team**—Bolan's famous Death Squad—battling urban savagery too brutal and volatile for regular law enforcement. And **Phoenix Force**—five extraordinary warriors handpicked by Bolan to fight the dirtiest of antiterrorist wars, blazing into even greater danger.

Fight alongside these three courageous forces for freedom in all-new action-packed novels! Travel to the gloomy depths of the cold Atlantic, the scorching sands of the Sahara, and the desolate Russian plains. You'll feel the pressure and excitement building page after page, with nonstop action that keeps you enthralled until the explosive conclusion!

Now you can have all the new Gold Eagle novels delivered right to your home!

You won't want to miss a single one of these exciting new action-adventures. And you don't have to! Just fill out and mail the card at right, and we'll enter your name in the Gold Eagle home subscription plan. You'll then receive six brand-new action-packed Gold Eagle books every other month, delivered right to your home! You'll get two Mack Bolan novels, one Able Team and one Phoenix Force, plus one book each from two thrilling, new Gold Eagle libraries, **SOBs** and **Track**. In **SOBs** you'll meet the legendary team of mercenary warriors who fight for justice and win. **Track** features a military and weapons genius on a mission to stop a maniac whose dream is everybody's worst nightmare. Only Track stands between us and nuclear hell!

FREE! The New War Book and Mack Bolan bumper sticker.

As soon as we receive your card we'll rush you the long-awaited New War Book and Mack Bolan bumper sticker—both ABSOLUTELY FREE. Then under separate cover, you'll receive your six Gold Eagle novels.

The New War Book is *packed* with exciting information for Bolan fans: a revealing look at the hero's life...two new short stories...book character biographies...even a combat catalog describing weapons used in the novels! The New War Book is a special collector's item you'll want to read again and again. And it's yours FREE when you mail your card!

Of course, you're under no obligation to buy anything. Your first six books come on a 10-day free trial—if you're not thrilled with them, just return them and owe nothing. The New War Book and bumper sticker are yours to keep, FREE!

Don't miss a single one of these thrilling novels...mail the card now, while you're thinking about it.

HE'S UNSTOPPABLE. AND HE'LL FIGHT TO DEFEND FREEDOM!

Mail this coupon today!